DATE DUE

	Level 4.3	Pi 760	

Books by Patricia Rushford

Young Adult Fiction

JENNIE McGRADY MYSTERIES

1. *Too Many Secrets*
2. *Silent Witness*
3. *Pursued*
4. *Deceived*
5. *Without a Trace*
6. *Dying to Win*
7. *Betrayed*
8. *In Too Deep*
9. *Over the Edge*
10. *From the Ashes*
11. *Desperate Measures*
12. *Abandoned*

Adult Fiction

Morningsong

HELEN BRADLEY MYSTERIES

1. *Now I Lay Me Down to Sleep*
2. *Red Sky in Mourning*
3. *A Haunting Refrain*

Dying To Win

Patricia H. Rushford

BETHANY HOUSE PUBLISHERS
MINNEAPOLIS, MINNESOTA 55438

Published by Bethany House Publishers
A Ministry of Bethany Fellowship International
11400 Hampshire Avenue South
Minneapolis, Minnesota 55438
www.bethanyhouse.com

Printed in the United States of America by
Bethany Press International
Minneapolis, Minnesota 55438

Library of Congress Catalog Number
95–33332

ISBN 1–55661–559–0

For David

PATRICIA RUSHFORD is an award-winning writer, speaker, and teacher who has published over twenty books and numerous articles, including *What Kids Need Most in a Mom*, *The Humpty Dumpty Syndrome: Putting Yourself Back Together Again*, and her first young adult novel, *Kristen's Choice*. She is a registered nurse and has a master's degree in counseling from Western Evangelical Seminary. She and her husband, Ron, live in Washington State and have two grown children, six grandchildren, and lots of nephews and nieces.

Pat has been reading mysteries for as long as she can remember and is delighted to be writing a series of her own. She is a member of Mystery Writers of America, Society of Children's Book Writers and Illustrators, and several other writing organizations. She is also co-director of Writer's Weekend at the Beach.

1

"Were you shocked to discover who had abducted the children?" Nancy Edwards, one of the television news reporters, directed her question to Jennie McGrady.

"Yes." *Of course I was*, Jennie wanted to say, but didn't. If she'd known who had taken the children, she'd have been able to rescue them immediately, instead of going through the terror of being abducted and nearly killed herself.

Jennie gazed out over the herd of reporters and cameras. She and her mother had been answering questions for over an hour. Her cobalt blue eyes had long since glazed over. Her jaw ached and Jennie figured it would probably take a week for her camera smile to fade.

Any other time Jennie might have enjoyed the media attention. She'd helped solve several criminal cases of late, and though she had no delusions of being an internationally known amateur detective, she did relish these brief snatches of fame. Now, however, she just wanted to go home.

Her excitement over rescuing her little brother, Nick, and his four-year-old friend, Hannah Stuart, had long since turned to exhaustion. Jennie lifted her long, nearly black hair from the back of her neck, wishing she'd braided it. She'd worn a white cotton dress, but the heat from the lights had turned the podium area into a sauna.

Susan McGrady slipped a comforting arm around her

daughter's waist. Her auburn hair tickled Jennie's chin. "We were all surprised, and disturbed," Mom said, her voice lacking expression. "We're also very tired. I think it would be a good idea to conclude the press conference." She glanced to her left where Nick and Hannah sat on separate chairs, both asleep and leaning against each other like limp rag dolls.

Several of the photographers followed her gaze. They must have thought the photo opportunity too great to pass up. For the next few seconds, lights flashed at the children, cameras popped and whirred, then focused back on Jennie and her mother.

"What's going to happen to Hannah?" another voice from the crowd asked.

"It's too soon to say," Mom answered. "Children's Services has granted me temporary custody."

Other questions erupted. Mom held up her hand and shook her head. "No more questions, please." She glanced up to meet Jennie's eyes. "Why don't you take Nick? I'll carry Hannah." Mom turned to Gram and J.B., who were seated behind them on the platform. "Would you mind finishing up here?" she whispered. "Give us a chance to escape?"

J.B., otherwise known as Jason Bradley, went to the microphone and motioned for Gram to join him. Jennie had come to love J.B., but still had trouble imagining the silver-haired Irish FBI agent as her grandfather. He seemed a more likely candidate for a James Bond movie. Actually, so did Gram. As a travel writer, ex-police officer, and part-time agent, Gram lived the kind of life others only dreamed about. Maybe that's what made them such a perfect couple—and just about the most interesting people Jennie knew.

Holding the press conference at the Hilton in downtown Portland had been J.B.'s idea. That way, he'd explained, they could answer all of the reporters' questions at one time. It had also given the family time to celebrate Nick and Hannah's homecoming privately.

"Ladies and gentlemen," J.B. began. With his Irish accent and firm, mellow voice, he appeased the crowd with a promise to answer a few more questions.

The thought of leaving revived Jennie. She tossed her grandparents a genuine smile and scooped Nick into her arms, then followed her mother through a side door. The door led to a hallway, which would eventually take them to the street and their car.

To guarantee their privacy, J.B. had arranged for security guards to be posted at the pressroom door as well as the hotel entrance. Halfway down the hall, Jennie heard a ruckus and turned around. Apparently, one of the reporters had decided to follow them because the guards blocked the doorway and were talking to a young man with a camera.

Jennie shook her head and continued. Reporters could be relentless. She'd nearly reached the exit when she heard footsteps behind her.

"How does it feel to be a hero, Jennie?"

She groaned and kept walking. "Don't you people know when to quit? The press conference is over. How did you get past security?"

"I told them I was your boyfriend." The reporter nearly ran into her when she stopped.

"My what?"

Nick moaned and turned his head, letting it come to rest on her left shoulder.

"Well, I am a friend—sort of."

The tall, lanky young man looked familiar, but her mind refused to come up with a name.

"Help me out here, Jen. This could be my big break."

"Gavin?" Jennie finally recognized him. Gavin Winslow worked on *The Forum*, Trinity High's school paper. He was forever following people around with his camera and tape recorder. "What are you doing here? School doesn't start for a month and a half. This story will be old news by then."

"I got a summer job with *The Oregonian*. So far I've only been able to do small stuff. When I told the editor I knew you personally, he gave me the assignment. He wants me to do a feature story on you and your little brother—you know, the human interest angle." Gavin reached up and brushed several strands of straight hair, almost as dark as her own, from his forehead. When he pushed his glasses back he reminded her of Clark Kent—without the muscle.

"Me?" she asked. Nick stirred in her arms again. Jennie shifted him to her right arm and supported some of his weight with her hip. "Why would you want to do a story about me? The press already knows more about me than I know about myself."

"You're a hero, Jennie. Two kids were kidnapped and you risked your own neck to save them. The boss wants your story."

Jennie rolled her eyes and started to walk away. "No way."

Gavin stepped in front of her. "Please, Jen. This is extremely important to me."

Exhaustion washed over her again. Seeing the disappointment in his blue-gray eyes, her reserve crumbled. "Okay," she heard herself say. "You can come by tomorrow afternoon."

"Great! I'll be there at one." Gavin's eyes flashed to high beam. "You won't regret this, McGrady."

Jennie watched as he loped off. Some of his excitement and exuberance had worn off on her and she found herself looking forward to the interview almost as much as she dreaded it.

2

When Jennie reached the sidewalk, her mother already had the car running and, thankfully, the air conditioner. She secured Nick into the seat belt beside Hannah and climbed into the front passenger seat of the Oldsmobile. Being in a car—any car—brought back memories of her dearly departed white Mustang. During the search for Nick, the car had tangled with some trees and lost.

"What took you so long?" Mom asked as she shifted into drive and pulled away from the curb. "I was about to send in reinforcements."

"I ran into a guy from school," Jennie answered, pushing away the depressing thoughts of losing her car. "He wants to interview me."

"You told him no, didn't you? We've had enough excitement for a while. I just hope those reporters don't decide to set up camp in our front yard." Mom stopped at a red light and glanced at Jennie. "You agreed to the interview?"

Jennie nodded, wishing she could avert the forthcoming lecture. "He's a friend, Mom. He goes to Trinity High *and* to our church."

"I don't care if he's the Pope." Mom sighed as the light turned green. Dividing her attention between the late Sunday afternoon traffic and Jennie, she began what promised to be a long lecture. "Honey, I know all this attention is exciting, but you have to know where to draw the line."

"I know. . . ." Jennie rubbed at the goosebumps on her bare arms and reached forward to turn the air conditioner down.

"It's not that I don't want you to talk to the press. You deserve the recognition. It's just that we . . ."

"We have to think of the children," Jennie finished.

Mom smiled. "Are you telling me I've said this before?"

"Only about a dozen times since yesterday. Don't worry so much, Mom. In another couple of days the press will move on to something else. Right now the kidnapping is big news. People want to know what happened. Tomorrow they won't remember our names."

Mom lifted her eyebrows in an I'll-believe-it-when-I-see-it look. "So, who's the *friend?*"

"Gavin Winslow."

"Really." Mom raised her eyebrows again. Tossing Jennie a conspiratorial smile she added, "Giving Ryan a little competition?"

"Mom, p-lease." Ryan Johnson, her long-time friend, lived next door to Gram in Bay Village on the Oregon Coast. Just when their relationship had begun to grow into something more interesting, Ryan decided to spend the summer fishing in Alaska to earn money for college. When he heard about Nick's disappearance, Ryan left his fishing job and flew to Portland to be with her.

With the kidnapping ordeal over, he'd gone back to the beach to spend a couple days with his mom and stepdad. He'd be back tomorrow and had promised her a real date—with dinner and a movie. Sadly, the following day she'd be dropping him off at the airport. Their on-and-off romance was definitely on at the moment and Jennie didn't want anything or anyone to get in the way.

She shook her head. "Trust me on this one. There is no way Gavin could compete with Ryan."

12

"Oh, I don't know. He's intelligent and rather good-looking, and, according to my source, he's going to be the next Peter Jennings."

Jennie didn't like the direction the conversation was heading. One of the problems with going to a private school was that parents usually knew one another and the kids. Mom's *source* was probably Gavin's mother. Jennie had no intention of dating anyone but Ryan, especially now that she knew how he felt about her.

"Speaking of someone being interested in someone," Jennie said, abruptly changing the subject, "are you and Michael getting back together?" Michael Rhodes was Mom's ex-fiancé. Jennie regretted asking the question the moment it came out of her mouth. "I mean, he came with you to pick us up at the hospital last night—I thought maybe—"

The teasing grin on Mom's face faded into a pained expression. She didn't answer.

"I'm sorry," Jennie said. "I shouldn't have brought it up."

"No, it's all right." Mom frowned and bit her lip. "We've decided it might be a good idea to see other people for a while. It was Michael's idea. He thought maybe dating others would help us evaluate how we really feel about each other."

"So are you going to?"

"Maybe."

The conversation stalemated as Jennie sank into her own thoughts and Mom into hers. Thinking about Mom and Michael naturally brought back memories of her father, Jason McGrady. He'd disappeared five years before in a mysterious plane crash. Jennie had never accepted the theory that he'd been killed, and on her sixteenth birthday decided it was time to solve the mystery of his disappearance once and for all. She'd managed to accomplish her goal, but the dream of seeing her parents reunited fizzled like a fire in a rainstorm.

Dad wasn't coming home.

As an agent for the Drug Enforcement Agency, he'd made

too many powerful enemies in the drug world. In order to protect himself and his family, he'd changed his identity. Jason McGrady no longer existed—the government had declared him officially dead. Only Jennie, Gram, and a few top-level officials knew the truth.

At first Jennie thought keeping Dad's secret would be easy. Now she wasn't so sure. Mom deserved to know. *But you made a promise, McGrady*, Jennie reminded herself.

She closed her eyes and pictured the last few moments she had shared with her father. A flood of emotions tumbled inside her like clothes in a dryer. She'd been so proud of him, bringing down drug lords and curbing drug traffic into the United States and abroad. At the same time, Jennie resented his absence—especially during the last few days.

You had to have known about Nick, she mentally accused him. Every television station and newspaper in the country had carried the story. *You should have been with us*. Jennie searched for excuses that would vindicate him, but could find none. She sighed. *Oh, Dad, why couldn't you have at least called? We needed you.*

"Are you okay, honey?" Mom asked as she reached over to take Jennie's hand in hers. "You look—I don't know—angry, sad."

"I was just wishing Dad could have been here."

Mom squeezed Jennie's hand. Tears gathered in her eyes. "I wish I knew what to say. You don't know how many times I've felt the same thing—even before the crash. He never seemed to be there when we needed him. I think the worst time was not having him with us when Nick was born."

Or when Nick was growing up, Jennie added silently, remembering the pain in Dad's eyes when he'd talked about the son he'd never known.

"I didn't feel that way this time," Mom continued. "Maybe because of Michael's support." Mom wiped the moisture from her cheeks with her fingers. "Mostly, though,

I think it's because I know now that your father's really gone. He was a good man, Jennie. In his own way he loved us."

Loves us, Mom, Jennie wanted to say, but couldn't. Dad did love them. She'd seen it in his face when he told her he couldn't go home. So why hadn't he called? *Because it's too dangerous, McGrady,* she reminded herself. *Dangerous for him and for the family.*

When they arrived at the house, Jennie pushed her disappointment and resentment away and helped her mother settle the children into bed to finish their naps. With the ordeal they had gone through, Jennie could have used a nap herself. Instead she decided to change clothes and read until dinner.

A few minutes later, wearing a comfortable oversized pink cotton T-shirt and knit white shorts, Jennie stretched out on one of the lounge chairs on the porch and began to read the new mystery she'd gotten from Gram.

Afternoon faded into dusk, then night. Somewhere in between, Nick and Hannah woke up and wanted to play dragons. They'd eaten a dinner of salad, spaghetti with meat sauce, and garlic bread, then watched the news. The hour-and-a-half interview had been condensed to a two-minute segment as the newscaster related a happy ending to a tragic story.

Ryan called at nine-thirty as dark clouds, hovering on the horizon, devoured the sun's last rays.

"How's the hero business?" Ryan teased when Jennie answered the private phone in her room. "Been offered any movie contracts yet?"

Jennie chuckled. "Sure. My agent and I are trying to decide between Spielberg and Disney. Then, of course, I have to find someone to play me."

"Oh, that's easy," Ryan said. "Connie Selleca."

"Really?" Jennie carried the phone to her dresser and studied herself in the mirror. She'd never seen herself as es-

15

pecially pretty. Compared to beauty contest winners like her redheaded cousin, Lisa, and their elegant and sophisticated friend, Allison Beaumont, Jennie considered herself average looking. But Ryan's comment made her feel attractive. With her long dark hair and cobalt blue eyes, she did resemble Connie—just a little.

"So tell me honestly," Ryan said, becoming more serious. "How are you doing? I caught the news earlier. You looked great, but I could tell you were pretty bummed out."

Jennie moved away from the mirror, wandered back to her bed, and sat down. "That's putting it mildly." She told him about the long press conference and the scheduled interview with Gavin Winslow. "Oh no. I just realized I have him coming about the same time you are."

"Hey, don't worry about it. Mom and I probably won't get to Portland until around two. If he's still there, I'll just come in and make faces at you."

They talked for another five minutes about friends, Alaska, and their date the next night, then hung up. Jennie spent the next hour or so at loose ends. She wandered around the house enjoying the quiet, yet wishing she could talk to someone. Mom, a CPA, was holed up in her office catching up on some paper work. After trying a few friends and finding no one at home, Jennie curled up on the couch and finished reading the book she'd started earlier.

She finished the book at eleven and went in search of her mother. Jennie found her, still in her office, hunched over a pile of ledgers. "Mom? I just wanted to let you know I'm going to bed."

Mom glanced at her watch and frowned. "I'll be up in a while. I just need to make a few more entries."

Jennie kissed Mom good-night and headed upstairs, stopping off at Nick's room to check on him and Hannah. She watched them for a few minutes and, not being able to resist, knelt beside Nick. She brushed his dark wavy hair aside and pressed her lips to his forehead. " 'Night, little buddy," she whispered.

Stopping at Hannah's temporary bed, Jennie gently removed a Madeline book. Eventually, Hannah would have her own room, but for now, Nick insisted on taking care of her.

With the back of her fingers she stroked Hannah's cheek, and sighed. An overwhelming feeling of sadness washed over her. "You're going to be all right, little one," Jennie promised. "We'll take good care of you."

Jennie rose to leave, pausing in the doorway to look back at the children she'd helped save. After sending up thanks for the umpteenth time, she closed the door.

Jennie brushed her teeth, changed into her lightweight cotton pajamas, and turned out the light. The room was stuffy and warm so she opened the windows, then sat in her window seat. Cool summer air wafted in, smelling of roses. She leaned against the cushions and watched the moon play hide-and-seek behind the clouds.

Tomorrow would be a busy day. She'd promised to help her mother clean the house, wash the car, and mow the lawn—all before Ryan came. She remembered her appointment with Gavin and groaned. Why had she agreed to it? Before she could think of a way out of the commitment, her phone rang. Jennie glanced at the clock. Eleven-thirty. Probably Lisa calling to let her know how things went.

"Hello?" Jennie answered, cradling the receiver against her shoulder.

No one answered.

"Lisa, is that you?"

Still no answer.

"Who is this? Look, I know you're there. I can hear you breathing."

"Um . . . Jennie, this is Courtney Evans. You probably don't remember me. I go to Trinity."

A picture of the tall slender girl appeared in Jennie's

mind. She and Courtney had a similar build, but there the resemblance ended. Courtney's short, shaggy haircut varied in color from cream to burgundy, depending on her mood. She wore colored contacts—green one day, purple the next. She must have had a dozen shades.

Courtney had been expelled from school twice for wearing "inappropriate dress." Her *dress* ranged from studded leathers with pants so tight they probably had to be peeled off, to layers of clothes that looked like rejects from a thrift store.

"Of course I remember you," Jennie said, hoping she didn't sound too critical.

"The reason, um . . . the reason I'm calling is . . . Look, never mind, I shouldn't have bothered you."

"No, hey, it's okay. Really."

"I saw you on the news tonight and thought maybe you could help. . . ." Courtney hesitated again. Jennie heard a shuddering sound and wondered if she'd been crying.

"Are you in some kind of trouble?"

"Yeah, I guess you could say that. Look, could you meet me at the mall tomorrow afternoon?"

"Tomorrow?" With Gavin coming—and her date with Ryan, there was no way. Still, Jennie couldn't ignore her plea for help. "Maybe late. I have an appointment. . . ."

"Right. Forget I called, okay? I shouldn't have bothered you."

"Courtney, wait. Courtney!"

3

Jennie had been kissing Ryan and suddenly his summer sky eyes faded to gray, glasses appeared on his blue face, and his hair turned dark.

"No! Go away and leave me alone." Jennie recognized the voice as her own as she fought her way out of the strange and annoying dream.

Gavin had been following her. No matter what she did, Gavin was there. Jennie tried to scream, but nothing came out. She tried to run, but her feet wouldn't move. Even in her sleep he sat beside her—watching. He kissed her hand—then licked it. Gross!

She shoved her wet hand under her pillow. "Leave me alone."

A snuffling, whining sound roused her more fully. Someone pulled at the sheets. She grabbed them back.

Wait a minute, McGrady. This isn't a dream. Someone's in your room. She yanked the covers off and bolted out of bed. Jennie fully expected to see the would-be reporter sitting in the chair, pad and pencil in hand, poised for an interview. The intruder, however, was not Gavin Winslow, but Nick's St. Bernard puppy. Sinking back onto the bed, Jennie willed her heart rate to settle back into its normal rhythm.

"Bernie." She ruffled the dog's silky brown and white fur. "Am I glad to see you. You would not believe the crazy dream I just had."

Remembering the interview she'd promised Gavin, Jennie grimaced. "I just hope he doesn't turn out to be that obnoxious in real life."

Bernie joined her on the bed and planted another slobbery kiss—this time on her face. A moment later he bounced to the door, turned around, woofed, then disappeared. When Jennie didn't follow, he came back in and looked up at her with huge, pleading brown eyes.

"Let me guess. You're hungry."

Bernie pulled in his tongue and stopped panting long enough to woof again, then headed for the door. Jennie glanced at the radio alarm beside her bed. Six a.m. "Why me?" She rolled her eyes and looked longingly at her pillow. "Mom bought you. You're Nick's responsibility. Okay, okay, I'm the only one who forgot to close my door."

Resigning herself to the task at hand, Jennie pulled on her bathrobe, then followed Bernie down the stairs and into the kitchen. At the pantry, Bernie stopped and let her get ahead of him. His tail swished wildly from one side to the other as she pulled open the bi-fold louvered doors and scooped about a pound of Puppy Chow from the 100-pound bag. "I'm surprised you haven't figured out a way to get into the pantry yet." When Jennie finished pouring the food, he nudged her out of the way and buried his nose into his dish.

She refilled his water bowl, then set a cup of water in the microwave for herself. While waiting for the water to heat, Jennie raided the refrigerator, surfaced with a carton of yogurt, and topped it with granola. A few minutes later, with tea and breakfast in hand, Jennie made her way back through the house and out the front door. She settled into the white porch swing to enjoy the freshness of the morning. A heavy rain had washed away the dust and summer heat.

Her annoyance at being awakened so early disappeared in an overwhelming sense of gratefulness. Off to the east the sun was just getting up. The clear rose-colored sky held a promise of a bright, new, wonderful day.

The children were safe, Ryan would be coming that afternoon, and Gavin's annoying presence had only been a dream.

On a slightly depressing note, the dream held a tinge of reality. Ryan would be leaving tomorrow. Jennie would be taking him to the airport where he'd catch a flight to Alaska for another month of fishing. She hated saying goodbye again, but at least this time she knew he loved her.

Jennie leaned her head back against the post and frowned as Ryan's image faded from her mind and Courtney Evans' face came into focus.

The disturbing phone call she'd gotten from Courtney last night drifted into her memory like a black cloud marring an otherwise clear day. She'd tried to call Courtney back right away, but no one answered.

Let it go, McGrady, she told herself firmly. *If it's really important she'll get hold of you. But what if she can't?* another part of her wondered. *What if she's in trouble?*

Okay, so maybe she wouldn't forget it. She'd try calling Courtney again later that morning. A greeting from the paper boy and the thump of *The Oregonian* hitting the porch step brought Jennie out of her reverie.

Jennie finished her yogurt and tea, scooped up the paper, and wandered back into the kitchen. She deposited the paper on the table and her breakfast dishes in the sink. By eight o'clock Jennie had gotten dressed, cleaned her room, done a load of laundry, and made breakfast—French toast, ham, and pineapple-orange juice for Mom and the kids. Mom stumbled into the kitchen just as the coffee machine sputtered its I'm-ready signal.

"Good morning, Mother," Jennie chirped. She set coffee and the morning paper on the table and steered her mother to the chair.

Mom stared at the table and yawned before lifting the cup

to her lips. "Okay," she mumbled, still holding the cup, "what have you done with my daughter?"

Jennie grinned. "Couldn't fool you, could we? I am an alien being. My spaceship landed in your backyard last night. We climbed through an open window and captured Jennie. My colleagues are extracting information from her brain as we speak. I have taken on her persona. My alien friends are likewise taking over the bodies of certain key people we see as highly intelligent beings. Soon we will rule the world."

"Highly intelligent beings? Taking over the world? Hmmm. That sounds plausible. For a moment I thought you were going to tell me you got up early, were in a good mood, and decided to make everyone breakfast."

"Not even I would have believed that story." Jennie dished up a plate of French toast and ham and served her mother. "There will be differences, Mrs. McGrady, but in time you will come to accept me. Now relax and enjoy your breakfast while I get Nick and Hannah up."

"We're already up, Jennie." Hannah appeared in the doorway, took her thumb out of her mouth to speak, then plugged it back in.

Nick raced past her and pulled out a chair. "You sit here, Hannah. This can be your place."

Hannah obediently climbed into the chair Nick indicated and watched intently as he took the one next to her. Jennie's throat tightened. She wondered how long the kidnapping would bother her. Swallowing back the rush of emotions, Jennie dished up their plates.

Nick shoveled a piece of French toast into his mouth. A trail of syrup ran down his chin; he tried to catch it with his tongue.

"Use your napkin," Mom said as she cut up Hannah's ham.

Jennie pulled out a chair and was about to lower herself into it.

Mom opened *The Oregonian* and almost spilled her coffee. "Did you see this?"

Jennie shook her head. "No, why?"

"The entire front page is dedicated to the kidnapping." Jennie peered over Mom's shoulder. Under the heading "He's Her Brother" was a large color photo of Jennie carrying Nick. The caption beneath the photo read, "Sixteen-year-old Jennie McGrady risks life to save abducted children."

"Here's an article by Gavin Winslow," Mom murmured.

Jennie leaned in closer. He wasn't interviewing her until this afternoon. Apparently, he'd written up the results of the press conference.

"He calls you 'a rising star in the field of law enforcement.' " Mom reached up and tucked a strand of hair behind Jennie's ear. "Sounds like you made quite an impression on him."

Embarrassed by the accolades, Jennie wrinkled her nose. "It doesn't take much to make an impression on Gavin."

Mom stood and took her dishes to the sink. "Oh, honey, stop being so cynical. Gavin seems like a nice young man. I'm not too crazy about him encouraging you with this law enforcement business though, *and* his tactics to get an interview might have been a little underhanded, but getting a story on the front page is impressive."

Jennie nodded. "I suppose you're right. I just hope the interview with him this afternoon is the end of it. Being a hero has its moments, but enough is enough."

After breakfast and dishes, Jennie volunteered to take the kids to the park so Mom could work. Being a CPA, she often met clients in their offices or had them come to her home. Mom sent Nick and Hannah up to clean Nick's room and began straightening the living room. "I hate to ask after all you've done this morning, Jennie, but how about vacuuming the downstairs for me?" Mom folded the afghan on the couch and fluffed a pink throw pillow. "I have a new client coming today. Frank Evans."

At the mention of his name, Jennie snapped to attention. "Frank Evans? Isn't that Courtney's dad?"

Mom nodded. "He's a pharmacist. Owns Evans' Pharmacy near Oregon City. A couple of Sundays ago, at church, he asked me if I'd do his books for him. His regular bookkeeper recently died."

Jennie considered telling her mother about Courtney's call, then decided against it. No point in alarming Mom or Courtney's father unnecessarily. "Um . . . when's he coming?"

"In an hour. I'd like to get the house cleaned—and I need to do some work in the office." She sighed and glanced around. "And I suppose I should shower and get dressed."

Glancing down at the tangle of shoulder-length auburn hair, Mom's bare feet, and the floral print cotton bathrobe, Jennie teased, "Why? You look great."

Mom cast Jennie an incredulous look. "Keep that up and I'll think you really are an alien."

Jennie chuckled as she retrieved the vacuum cleaner from the hall closet. Mom disappeared upstairs and Jennie wondered what, if anything, she should say to Mr. Evans. She had tried calling Courtney earlier and left a message on the answering machine. Jennie finally decided a few innocuous questions like, "How's Courtney?" wouldn't hurt.

Unfortunately, she didn't get to talk to him. Mom shooed Jennie, Nick, and Hannah out of the house half an hour before his arrival so she could "tidy her office." Judging from her mother's nervous behavior and the careful way she'd applied her makeup, Jennie had the unsettling feeling Mom viewed Frank Evans as more than just a client.

Jennie didn't much like the idea of her mother dating. After finding and talking with Dad, Jennie had been nearly ready to accept Michael as a stepfather. In her heart, she preferred having Mom and Dad get back together, but like Dad had said, "Things don't always work out the way you want them to."

Two hours later, Jennie extracted Nick and Hannah from the playground equipment and headed home. When the weary children lagged behind, Jennie suggested piggyback rides, which brought an immediate round of cheers. Since she had only one back, Nick did the gentlemanly thing and offered to let Hannah ride on Jennie while he walked Bernie.

Bernie, probably more interested in food than his family, strained at his leash as they neared the house. Jennie picked up her pace as well when she saw a teal green Lexus still parked in the driveway.

"Looks like Mom's client is still there," Jennie said to no one in particular as they neared the yard.

"What's a kwient?" Hannah asked.

Jennie was about to respond when the door opened and Mr. Evans and Mom stepped onto the porch. They were laughing. "Well," Frank said, "I'd better get back to work. I left Courtney in charge. She's a great help, but with that new look of hers I'm afraid she might scare off some of my more conservative customers. I guess I'll see you Friday night." He leaned toward Susan slightly, as if he were thinking about kissing her.

No, don't let him, Mom, please, you can't, Jennie wanted to yell, but didn't. Suddenly feeling confused and angry, she wanted to stop whatever was happening between Mr. Evans and her mother.

"Mommy, Mommy, guess what we did?" Nick raced across the yard and bounded up the steps.

Mr. Evans stepped back, then cleared his throat and smiled. Bending at the waist, he ruffled Nick's dark hair. "You must be Nick."

Nick backed away and wrapped his arms around Mom's leg.

"Jennie," Hannah whispered in Jennie's ear. "Don't squeeze me so hard."

"Oh, Hannah, I'm sorry." Jennie released her grip on Hannah's legs and lowered her to the ground. "Did I hurt you?"

Hannah shook her head, rubbing her blond curls against Jennie's arm.

With Hannah clinging to her hand, Jennie walked toward the steps. "Hi, Mr. Evans." She shoved her confused emotions temporarily aside. "I'm Jennie."

"I know. I was just telling your mother that I wished you and Courtney could get together. You'd be a good influence on her, I . . ." His voice trailed off.

Oh, great. Just what she always wanted to be—an influence. Was that why Courtney had called? Had her dad been bugging her about her choice of friends? No, being bugged didn't explain the fear Jennie had sensed in Courtney's voice.

"Maybe we could have you and Courtney over for dinner one night," Mom said, interrupting Jennie's thoughts. "That would give the girls a chance to get to know each other."

"Wonderful idea, Susan. I'll talk to Courtney." Mr. Evans turned back to Jennie. "Courtney's really a sweet girl—at least she was before . . ." he paused and glanced at Mom, then at Nick and Hannah. "I think perhaps I'd better save that story for another time."

Frank Evans said goodbye and left. Whatever he'd been about to say couldn't be said in front of the children. Jennie felt like she'd come to the end of a suspenseful chapter in a mystery, only to find someone had torn out the rest of the pages.

4

Over a lunch of toasted cheese sandwiches, tomato soup, and Jell-O, Jennie brooded about Courtney's phone call and Mr. Evans' unfinished sentence.

"You'll never guess who called while you were out," Mom said when they were nearly finished eating.

"Lisa?"

Mom shook her head. "Don't slurp your soup, Nick. Use your spoon."

"Courtney?"

"No. Marge Thurman, from the insurance company."

Jennie's thoughts about Courtney and her dad vanished. Marge would only be calling about one thing. Her car.

Jennie felt a twinge of sadness over losing the white Mustang. Being run off the road and landing in a stand of fir trees had done terrible things to it. Jennie had fought to have it restored, but the insurance adjuster insisted the car be totaled. "What did she say?"

"She's found a car for us."

Jennie frowned. "I don't understand. I thought they were just going to send us a check."

"Ordinarily they would, but with all we were going through, Marge offered to go a step further. She knew how much you liked the Mustang and said she'd do her best to find one like it."

"Really?" Jennie wiped her hands off on the napkin. "When do I get to see it?"

A horn sounded outside. Mom glanced at her watch, and the smile on her face broadened. "I think that's her."

Jennie excused herself and ran outside. Parked in the driveway was the most beautiful car she had ever seen. Marge Thurman stepped out and waved. "Do you like it? It's three years newer. I know the other one was white, but when I saw this one . . ."

"I love it." Jennie crossed behind the car, touching the glossy fire-engine red finish as she made her way to the driver's side.

Mom appeared on the porch with Nick and Hannah. "It looks expensive. Are you sure the insurance money will cover it?"

"Absolutely," Marge assured. "It was recently repossessed, so we got a great buy on it."

Another car, this one a cream-colored Cadillac, pulled into the driveway. "My husband," Marge explained, dropping the keys into Jennie's hand. "The papers are in the glove box." She patted the Mustang's trunk. "It's all yours, Jennie."

"Thanks!" Jennie resisted the urge to bounce as she gripped the keys. She waved goodbye and turned back to the car. Excitement pulsed through her, probably sending her adrenaline to dangerously high levels. Climbing into the driver's seat, she felt like a princess who'd just had a visit from her fairy godmother. "Wow," she murmured, running her hand over the black leather seats. "Radio, tape deck, air conditioner—everything."

Remembering the rest of her family, Jennie got out, leaned her arms on the roof, and offered them a ride.

"I'd love to, hon, but I think it will have to wait." Mom glanced toward the street. "Here comes Gavin. Maybe he'd like to go with you."

Images of the dream she'd had that morning threatened to cloud her day. *Come on, McGrady. Be fair. You promised Gavin an interview. You can enjoy driving the car later—with Ryan.*

Jennie took a deep breath and managed a smile as Gavin jumped off his bike, removed his helmet, and walked toward her. Bony legs extended from a pair of khaki shorts. His hair had a funny kink in it where the helmet had crushed it and his white polo shirt looked like he'd taken a shower with his clothes on. On his back he carried a dull reddish brown leather backpack that looked like it had survived a war.

After introducing Gavin to her new car and her family, Jennie offered him a seat in one of the wicker chairs adorning the front porch.

"Would you like something to drink?" Mom asked. "We have iced tea, lemonade, root beer, Coke. . . ."

"Thanks, Mrs. McGrady, but I'd prefer some ice water." He nodded toward his bike. "And maybe I could wash up?"

Jennie fixed a tray of drinks and dug some chocolate chip cookies out of the ceramic lamb cookie jar. She set them on the white wicker table. While she waited for Gavin, she imagined herself and Ryan driving through the woods.

"Bet you're anxious to drive it," Gavin said, pulling Jennie out of her daydream.

"I am. But . . .". Jennie glanced back at Gavin, surprised at the transformation. He'd changed his shirt and now wore a salmon-colored polo. He'd wet and combed his hair and looked—well, almost handsome.

"The interview?" Gavin grinned. "We can do that anywhere."

"Really?"

"Sure." He reached for his water and gulped it down to nothing but ice.

Jennie didn't need any more encouragement. After telling her mother where they were going, she and Gavin climbed into the car and headed west. With the windows down and the radio on, Jennie took the nearest route to Washington Park.

"So, do you want to interview me while I'm driving?"

"Yeah. Why don't you start by telling me your life story?"

"Not much to tell." Jennie started with what she thought was the most interesting part. About being born into a family of law-enforcement people. How her grandfather Ian—Gram's first husband—was a secret service agent, and had been killed in a bombing in Beruit. How her father had been a DEA agent prior to the plane crash. How her parents and Lisa's parents got together. "My mom's brother, Kevin Calhoun, is Lisa's dad—you know Lisa, don't you?"

When Gavin nodded, she went on. "Anyway, Dad and Uncle Kevin met in the Air Force—they were both pilots. When they got out, they stayed friends. Kevin fell in love with my dad's twin sister, Kate, and Dad fell in love with Kevin's younger sister, my mom. They had a double wedding a few months later."

"Whew," Gavin shook his head. "Sounds confusing."

"We're used to it." When Jennie's gaze met his he quickly glanced away, as if embarrassed at being caught. But at what? Looking at her? Jennie hoped that by agreeing to the interview or taking him for a drive he wouldn't think she was leading him on.

She sneaked a peek at him again, and this time it was her turn to be embarrassed. He'd been watching the road, then turned to catch her watching him.

He pressed his wire-framed glasses against his nose. "Driving around has been fun, Jennie, but do you think we could stop somewhere so I can get some photos? Also, I need part of the interview on tape."

Jennie parked in a wooded lot and she and Gavin found a shady spot near a pond. Once they were seated on the cool lawn, Gavin retrieved his camera, a tape recorder, and a notepad from the worn leather pack and began his interview.

After a few dozen photos and what seemed like a hundred questions later, Jennie called a halt to the interview. As they walked back to the car, she told him about Ryan and how he'd helped her in the kidnapping case.

"He sounds like a great guy. I'd like to meet him. Maybe I could ask him a few questions too." Gavin set his backpack down and folded himself into the passenger seat.

Gavin's response settled Jennie's mind about his possibly being interested in her as a girlfriend. She was beginning to feel much more at ease with him. "I'm sure Ryan won't mind." Jennie started the Mustang and shifted into reverse.

As she drove through the park and merged onto the Sunset Highway, an idea began to take shape and form. Being a reporter, Gavin just might be able to answer some of the questions she had about Courtney Evans. The trick would be to extract that information without arousing suspicion. "You're a good interviewer, Gavin."

"Thanks. You're an easy person to interview. Actually, it's my favorite part of being a reporter. I love to talk to people and listen to their stories."

"Have you ever interviewed Courtney Evans?" *Way to go, McGrady. So much for the subtle approach.*

Gavin frowned. "Courtney?"

Jennie had struck a nerve. She could almost see a wall go up between them. He seemed agitated. Why?

"Yeah," Jennie continued on as if she hadn't noticed his discomfort. "You must know her. It would be hard for anyone not to. She's one of the most, um . . . interesting kids in school."

"I know her." Gavin pushed a hand through his hair. "Why are you asking?"

Should she tell him about the phone call? Jennie played a mental tug-of-war with herself for a few seconds before coming to a decision. "Courtney called me last night and asked for my help. She wanted to meet me at the mall today. When I tried to explain that I had an appointment, she said to forget it and hung up. I tried calling her back, but . . ."

Gavin shook his head. "I wouldn't worry too much about it, Jennie. Courtney tends to be sort of melodramatic. And to answer your question, I did interview her—last May. You didn't see my article in *The Forum*?"

"No, I'm sorry. With finals and everything—I was getting ready for a trip to Florida with my grandmother."

"It was one of my best pieces. I titled it "Rainbow Girl" because of how she's always changing the color of her hair and eyes. A lot of people don't understand Courtney."

"She's not easy to understand. Those outrageous clothes and hairstyles. And her attitude—like she'd rather eat nails than talk to you. That's why I was so surprised when she called."

"You want to know about Courtney? Why don't you read the article I wrote? That will give you a better picture than anything I could say right now."

"You sound like you're upset with her about something."

Gavin folded his arms over his chest and sulked. After a few seconds he straightened and sighed. "You'll find out anyway, so I might as well tell you. After I interviewed her, Courtney and I became friends—we dated a few times. I thought we had something going, you know? After the article came out, she went from being an outsider to being Miss Popularity. Then she dumped me for a jock."

"Anyone I know?"

"Everyone in town knows him. Joel Nielsen."

Jennie raised her eyebrows. Joel would be a senior this year. He was captain of the football team and Brad's best friend. In a way, Jennie could understand Courtney's choice.

"I'm sorry, Gavin."

"I don't know. I should be used to it by now. It doesn't matter how intelligent or talented you are in this world. If you don't have a great *bod*, you might as well pack it in."

"Not all girls feel that way." Jennie pulled into the driveway. Ryan was there—stretched out on the chaise lounge on her front porch. "That's Ryan," Jennie said, a smile stretched across her face.

Jennie and Ryan talked with Gavin for about an hour. When Gavin left, Jennie was certain he felt better about himself. She gave Ryan credit for that. Not being much of a jock himself, Ryan had empathized with Gavin, then encouraged him to be himself.

"Eventually," Ryan said as they walked Gavin to his bike, "you'll find a girl who appreciates you."

Gavin snorted. "Sounds like something my mother would say."

Ryan laughed. "It is. My mother told me that all through my freshman and sophomore years. Turned out to be right." Ryan settled his arm around Jennie's shoulder and hugged her to him. "Case in point," he said, looking square into Jennie's eyes. "You can't do much better than this."

Wow. The butterflies in Jennie's stomach took off at warp speed. When Ryan looked away, Jennie let her focus shift back to Gavin.

He snapped the chin strap of his helmet into place and shrugged on his backpack. Looking from Ryan to Jennie, he said, "Thanks again for the interview. I'll bring a copy of the article by tomorrow afternoon."

Jennie agreed, but the moment Gavin's bike disappeared around the corner of Magnolia and Elm, she forgot he even existed. Her long-awaited date with Ryan had officially begun.

5

On Tuesday morning, Jennie overslept.

She managed to get Ryan to the airport twenty minutes before his flight. Just time enough to drop him off at the curb and say goodbye. "I'll miss you," she whispered in his ear when he hugged her.

"Me too." Ryan chuckled. "I mean . . . I won't miss me. I'll miss you." He released her and took a step back. "Hey, promise me you'll stay out of trouble while I'm gone."

Jennie laughed. "I'll try." She waved goodbye until he disappeared through the revolving door. She hated seeing Ryan go, but he'd be back in four weeks.

Stay out of trouble? He was teasing, but also serious. Jennie wondered what Ryan would have said if she'd told him about Courtney.

On the way home, she stopped by Lisa's. It seemed odd that Lisa hadn't called after her date with Brad. In fact, Jennie hadn't seen or talked to her cousin since Friday—nearly four days ago. Up until now Jennie had been too busy to worry. Lisa usually kept her informed of everything from the latest happenings around town to her newest nail color. So why hadn't she called?

When no one answered the door of the two-story English Tudor, Jennie wandered around to the back of the house to Aunt Kate's studio where she did her artwork and conducted her interior-design business. The door was unlocked so Jennie went in.

She loved the wild splashes of color and natural light streaming in from the skylights and large picture windows. The scent of plum potpourri mingled with linseed oil, paint, and a touch of turpentine. On an easel in the middle of the room sat an unfinished portrait of Gram and J.B. Jennie hadn't seen it before and marveled at how lifelike Kate had made them. The silver in Gram's salt-and-pepper hair glistened in the light. Jennie wondered if Kate was doing it as a wedding present for them.

Jennie knocked on the bedroom door before opening it. Gram and J.B. had been staying there the last few nights and she hoped Gram would be there. She wasn't. Jennie left a note on the front door of the main house asking Lisa to call or come over, then headed home.

Jennie felt the chaos the moment she walked in the front door. Four large mailbags cluttered the entry, their contents spilling out onto the tiled floor.

Nick and Hannah charged at her, nearly knocking her over.

"Look at all the mail, Jennie," Nick cheered. "We got lots and lots, and Mommy's pulling her hair out."

Mom appeared in the kitchen doorway, her thick auburn tresses still intact. "Thank goodness you're back. The phone hasn't stopped ringing since you left."

"What's going on?"

"These, for one thing." Mom pointed to the mail. "I started going through them and gave up. Kate and Lisa are coming by later to help out. And I've taken about twenty phone calls asking for you."

"When is Lisa coming? I stopped by the house on my way home, but no one was there."

"I'm not sure—Kate said something about a doctor appointment. Apparently Lisa's not been feeling well."

Jennie frowned, concern over her cousin's health mingled with relief that she'd be seeing her soon.

Mom handed her a notepad with two pages full of names and numbers. "I was tempted to just say no to most of these. But I decided you might want to do that yourself."

Jennie glanced at the list. "Someone wants me to help them find their dog?"

Mom smiled. "That's only the beginning. Dogs, birds, cats, jewelry, and—" she paused. "One woman thought you might be able to help her locate her missing child." Tears filled her gray-green eyes. "I almost feel guilty at our success in finding Nick so quickly. I wish there was something we could do for them."

"Maybe I could—"

"No," Mom interrupted. "Despite what the media says, you are not a detective. You attract enough trouble on your own without looking for it."

Jennie wanted to argue the point, but didn't. After what she and her family had just been through, she wasn't in the mood to do anything remotely dangerous.

"Besides," Mom went on. "I doubt any of us can help in this case. It's been over three years since her child disappeared."

"Oh, Mom, that's so sad." Jennie looked down at the list again. "What am I supposed to tell all these people? That my mother won't let me help them?"

"Sounds good to me."

Jennie had gotten halfway through the list when Aunt Kate and Lisa arrived.

"Just don't, okay?" Jennie heard Lisa say before they entered the kitchen.

Don't what? Jennie wanted to ask, but didn't. She'd find out later. Aunt Kate appeared first, giving Mom, then Jennie a hug. "Where do you want us, Susan?" Kate reached into the cupboard and retrieved a cup, then poured herself some coffee.

Watching Aunt Kate was like looking in the mirror—not unusual when you considered the fact that Kate was Dad's twin and that Jennie carried the McGrady genes. People were always confusing them as mother and daughter. Today, they looked almost like twins—both wore white shorts and shirts with their long, dark hair in ponytails.

Lisa, on the other hand, looked like Mom—flaming red hair, freckles, short, with a great figure. At least she used to. Jennie shifted her focus from Kate to Lisa, and felt like she'd been punched in the stomach. Lisa's beautiful round face was now pale and gaunt. Deep shadows lined her once sparkling green eyes. She looked sick—really sick.

Concern and shock coiled themselves around Jennie's heart. "Lisa, what's wrong? You look awful."

"Thanks a lot," she countered, then offered a wane smile. She threw her mother a warning glance.

Aunt Kate sighed. "Lisa, honey, tell them. They know something is wrong and they're just going to think the worst."

"I can't." Lisa sank into a kitchen chair and stared at her clasped hands. "I should have known it would be impossible to keep a secret in this family."

Jennie's heart ached as her brain came up with the worst possible explanation. Tears formed in her eyes. "It's cancer, isn't it? Is that why you won't tell us?"

"No. It's . . ." Lisa glanced up at her mom. "You tell them."

Kate took a sip of her coffee. "Lisa is anorexic."

"What?" Jennie and her mother chorused.

Jennie rushed to her cousin's side and dropped into the chair next to her. "I can't believe that. You seemed fine last week."

Lisa continued to stare at her hands. "I was getting too fat. I decided to go on a diet after school let out in May—

while you were in Florida with Gram. At first everything went great. I lost five pounds for the cruise and felt so good I decided to keep going."

Jennie had noticed the weight loss, but hadn't thought much about it. Lisa often dieted for a week or two at a time, but had never been obsessive about it. "Going on a diet once in a while doesn't make you anorexic." Jennie glanced at Kate. "Does it?"

"No. And she doesn't have the chronic type—at least not yet. But she took her dieting too far this time." Kate slid a hand across Lisa's back, then let it come to rest on her shoulder. "The doctor said that she's messed up her electrolytes and metabolism. It's all very complicated, but the dieting along with not eating proper meals have worn her out. That last flu bug she got made matters even worse. Anyway, the good news is she's going to be okay."

"Don't look at me like that." Lisa glared at Jennie for a moment then glanced away. "I didn't mean to. I tried to stop." She folded her arms across her chest. "Anyway, you don't know what it's like to be overweight. You never have to worry about whether or not guys are going to like you."

"Lisa, I don't get it. You're not fat. You never have been. I've always thought of you as the pretty one with a gorgeous figure and you've always had dates. I'm a stick. I haven't even graduated to a B cup." Jennie stopped. *Way to go, McGrady,* she chastised herself. *She really wants to be reminded of how thin you are.*

"I just wanted to look good for the summer and—" Lisa paused to look up at Jennie. "Cheerleader tryouts are coming up. I knew I wouldn't make the rally squad unless I dropped some weight."

"Lisa, you need to forget about rally squad." Kate picked up her coffee cup. "The doctor said no strenuous activity for two weeks."

Mom put an arm around Lisa's shoulders. "I know exactly what you're going through. I've struggled with my weight too."

Lisa was crying now. "I don't want to die, Aunt Susan." She wrapped her arms around Mom's neck. "But I hate this."

"I know, honey, I know." Mom held Lisa close and patted her back.

Jennie had never seen this side of Lisa and it unnerved her. Her cousin had always been so bubbly and cheerful. As she thought back on it, looking good had always been important to Lisa. Jennie just hadn't realized how important until now.

Aunt Kate signaled to Jennie to follow her out of the kitchen. "I think it might be better if we let your mom handle this one," she whispered when they reached the entry. "I've been trying to get Lisa over here for two days. If anyone can help her through this, Susan can. I've tried to be supportive, but I have a hard time understanding why she's so down on herself."

Jennie nodded. "I feel terrible. Why couldn't I see it? I might have been able to help."

"I missed it too. I knew she'd dropped some weight, but it wasn't until she got the flu last week that I really noticed how frail she'd become." Kate sighed and offered Jennie a halfhearted smile. "But don't worry. She'll come out of it. I think there's just been too much going on lately, her breakup with Brad, the cruise, getting ready for cheerleading . . . at any rate, I think Lisa's weight loss has a lot to do with Brad."

"Lisa never called me to let me know how their date went. Do you know?"

Kate shrugged, then stooped to grab one of the mail bags and drag it into the dining room. "Ugh. You could get a hernia toting these things around." She scooped out a bunch of mail and sat in one of the six chairs surrounding the large antique rosewood table.

Jennie brought in the other bag and, following Kate's lead, began opening the mail.

"I'm not avoiding your question," Kate said, finally. "I don't really know. According to Lisa, everything is fine and she and Brad are going out again this Friday."

"You say that like you don't believe her."

"It's an intuition thing, you know. Something just doesn't feel right. I'm sure part of it is the way the anorexia has altered her personality. I have a feeling something else is going on. Maybe she'll tell you."

Kate paused to read the card she'd opened. "Oh, this is so nice. It's a congratulations card and there's a check for fifty dollars enclosed to help with expenses for Hannah."

Jennie hoped Lisa would talk to her, but a wall of secrecy had somehow come between them. They no longer told each other everything. *Later, McGrady*, Jennie promised herself. *Later you and Lisa will go up to your room and talk. It will be just like always. After all, you and Lisa are more than cousins— you're best friends*. That hadn't changed, had it?

Jennie set aside her nagging doubts and opened an envelope. She read the note and set it in the discard pile. It was from a guy in Minnesota asking her to marry him. This hero business was definitely turning into a major pain.

By the time Mom and Lisa joined them, Jennie and Aunt Kate had sorted through at least a hundred pieces of mail. Several people asked for Jennie's help in locating missing family members and animals. Most offered congratulations and encouragement. A few sent money.

Neither Lisa nor Mom brought up Lisa's problem, but Jennie hoped Lisa would still confide in her. She had a lot of questions and even more concerns.

———

They spent the entire afternoon opening and responding to the mail. At five, Mom called it to a halt and suggested they all go out for pizza. While Kate called Uncle Kevin, Jennie invited Lisa upstairs.

Lisa fell onto Jennie's bed, grabbing a fluffy white stuffed bunny as she went down. Jennie curled up on the window seat and leaned her head against the window. Neither of them spoke.

After about five minutes, Lisa broke the silence. "You think I'm a total nut case, don't you."

"I think . . ." Jennie began, weighing her words carefully. Then deciding to be honest, said, "Yes. I can't believe you would starve yourself like that. I thought you knew better."

"I don't have to listen to a lecture from you too, do I?" Lisa twisted around to a sitting position and stroked the bunny's ears. The beginnings of a smile appeared on her lips, then faded.

"I wish you had told me what was going on." Jennie left the window seat and plopped down on the bed next to Lisa.

"What would you have said if I had?"

"I'd have tried to talk you out of it."

"That's why I didn't say anything. I didn't want anybody to tell me I looked okay. I didn't feel okay."

"Does Brad have anything to do with this?"

Lisa hugged the fluffy bunny to her chest. "Before we broke up, he told me I could stand to lose a little weight. He wanted me to start working out so I could exchange my flab for muscle."

"Let me guess. You told him where he could take his muscle."

The semi-smile came back. "He really hurt me. I know he was just trying to be helpful, but it tore me up inside. He might as well have said, 'Lisa, you're a fat slob. Lose the weight or lose me.' "

"He didn't say that, did he?"

"Not exactly, but I knew what he meant. I got mad and broke up with him before he could dump me."

"Is that when you decided to go on this diet?"

Lisa tipped her head back and closed her eyes. "I didn't mean to lose so much. It just felt so good to be skinny. Then everything backfired. I started getting sick and . . ." Lisa's large green eyes reminded Jennie of pictures she'd seen of starving children. "The most frustrating part about all this is that now Brad thinks I'm too skinny. He liked me better the way I was." Her eyes turned to liquid pools and she looked away.

Jennie hooked an arm around Lisa's neck. "I take it your date with Brad didn't go so well. Is that why you didn't call me?"

"I tried to call, but your line was busy. Then I fell asleep. We worked things out. He apologized for making me think I was fat. When I get some strength back, he wants to help me with a weight-training program. He's taking me to a health-food store Friday before we go to a movie. Wants to show me some high-powered protein stuff."

"Sounds like he's turning into a health nut."

"He is. The whole football team is—especially Joel Nielsen. And it's really paying off for them. They are looking so good. In fact, Coach Haskell says if they play as well in the season as they do in practice, we may win the state championship." Lisa smiled again and this time it reached her eyes.

"By the way," Lisa said, becoming more animated, as though someone had wound her up. Jennie hoped it was a good sign. "Joel and Courtney asked about you the other night."

"What?" Jennie's attention snapped from Lisa's health to Courtney's name.

Lisa leaned back and frowned at Jennie's reaction. "It wasn't anything bad. They wanted to know about the cases you'd solved and—"

"When did you talk to Courtney?"

"Sunday night. Brad and I doubled with her and Joel. Why?"

Jennie told Lisa about the strange call she'd gotten, then asked, "Did she seem upset about anything? Do you know why she called?"

Lisa shook her head. "She seemed fine—a little crabby, but then that's Courtney. If she was in some kind of trouble, she didn't tell me about it. Courtney is so cool. I wish I had the nerve to do some of the stuff she does. I mean, Sunday night she had purple hair. And she wore these lavender contacts. The most bizarre thing I've done lately is wear green nail polish."

"Hmmm," Jennie murmured, not really listening. "That call is really bugging me. I left several messages, but she hasn't called me back. It's weird."

"Hey, look, I'll ask her about it Friday night. We're doubling again—or, better yet, you can ask her yourself at cheerleading tryouts tomorrow."

"Yeah, I will." Jennie thought again about the desperation she'd sensed in Courtney's voice. "I just hope it isn't too late."

6

It took several seconds for Jennie to digest Lisa's words. The statement, "You can ask her yourself at cheerleading tryouts" held more hidden messages than a "Where's Waldo" picture. First, of course, Courtney planned to be there. Second, Lisa wanted Jennie to come and had used Courtney as an enticement.

Nothing short of curiosity and a chance to talk to Courtney could have dragged Jennie to cheerleader tryouts and Lisa knew it. Not that Jennie had anything against cheerleaders, she just didn't feel coordinated enough to be one. Besides, Jennie really didn't see herself as the cheerleader type.

The third and probably scariest message was that, despite orders from her doctor and mother, Lisa intended to go ahead with the tryouts.

It was this point Jennie addressed first. "You're still going? Your mom said you were supposed to rest for at least two weeks."

"I will—after." Lisa wove a long strand of hair between perfectly manicured fingers. "Don't say it, Jen. And don't tell Mom. I've made up my mind. I've been resting for four days now. I've been thinking about this and I can do it."

"I don't believe you." Jennie placed her hand on Lisa's forehead. "This diet you were on has affected your brain.

You're delirious. Cheerleading is way too strenuous for you right now."

Lisa knocked Jennie's hand away. "I have to try. You can understand that. And I'll make it, you'll see." Lisa's gaze drifted up to meet Jennie's. "Please don't rat on me, Jen. If you love me at all, you'll let me do this. I can rest later. I just have to make the rally squad."

Jennie closed her eyes. *If you really love her,* a voice seemed to say, *you'll go downstairs right now and tell Aunt Kate.* Jennie didn't move. She did love Lisa, but—

Lisa placed a hand on Jennie's arm. "Please. This is extremely important to me. I'd do it for you."

"All right," Jennie heard herself saying. "I won't say anything right now. But I'm going with you and if I think for one second you're getting worse, I'll stop you myself."

"It'll be fine," Lisa promised. "I'll eat plenty of carbs and protein."

"Jennie," Mom's voice bellowed up the stairs. "Someone's here to see you."

"You expecting company?" Lisa asked.

Jennie glanced at her watch as if it might tell her something more than the time. "It's probably Gavin. He promised to show me the article he's writing about me."

Coming down the stairs, Jennie heard her mother invite Gavin to have pizza with them.

"That'd be great, Mrs. McGrady." He glanced up. "That is, if it's okay with Jennie."

It wasn't, but Jennie shrugged and said, "Sure, why not?" Gavin's presence bugged her, and Jennie wasn't sure why. After mulling it over a few seconds, she blamed the dream.

Though Gavin hadn't replaced Ryan in real life as he had in the dream, he had managed to insert himself into her life like an unwanted bout with poison oak.

"I brought you a copy of 'Rainbow Girl,' the article I did on Courtney," he said, drawing a clipping out of his worn backpack. "In case you lost your copy."

"Thanks." Her annoyance slinked away as she scanned Gavin's article.

"Jennie," her mother interrupted, "why don't you read it later. We need to get going."

Rather than leave the article until later, Jennie took it with her. Sitting between Lisa and Gavin in the rear seat of Aunt Kate's van, she finished reading about Courtney Evans. Okay, so reading when she should have been talking to Gavin and Lisa was rude, but Jennie couldn't wait. She hoped the article would give her some clues about Courtney and the strange phone call.

She browsed through some of the initial statistics and history. Up until the first of the year Courtney had lived in Boston. *After Mom died last year,* Gavin quoted her as saying, *my father decided to move to Oregon. I guess he thought we could leave the past behind. You can't, you know. Mom's dead. She'll always be dead. Nothing's going to change that.*

Jennie bit back the urge to cry. She thought back to the comment Mr. Evans had left unfinished the other day and filled it in. *Courtney's really a sweet girl—at least she was before . . . her mother died.* Having her mom die must have been really hard on her. No wonder she had problems.

Turning her attention back to the article, Jennie read Gavin's next question. *Why do you always change the color of your eyes and hair?* Courtney responded with, *My mom loved rainbows. She always used to tell me that rainbows were a sign of hope. In fact, she even called me her rainbow girl because she'd almost given up hope of ever having a child.*

Then I came along—I'm adopted. Courtney Hope Evans, that's me. I don't know, maybe I do it to drive my dad crazy. Maybe I do it for attention. Maybe I just do it to find the hope in me.

The article ended there. Jennie looked over at Gavin. "This is really good."

He shrugged and glanced away as if the compliment had embarrassed him. "Thanks."

The article revealed a lot about Courtney Evans, but it also told a great deal about Gavin Winslow. He was a talented writer. Jennie felt much of her annoyance toward him melt into admiration.

After their pizza dinner, Kate and Lisa dropped Jennie, Gavin, and the rest of Jennie's family off at the house and went home. Lisa had been strangely sullen the entire evening. Was she upset about something, or had the day's activities simply worn her out? Jennie's goodbye to Lisa included a brief hug and a warning to be careful.

Lisa answered with the standard, "Don't worry," and a look that said, *Don't tell.*

Once inside, Mom started to take the kids upstairs to get them ready for bed.

"We want Jennie to read us a story," Nick declared halfway up the stairs. "Will you? Please!"

"Jennie has company tonight," Mom said. "Maybe she can read to you tomorrow."

"Hey," Gavin piped up, "don't change your routine on my account. Maybe we can read to the kids together. I don't mind."

"Yeah!" Hannah and Nick both squealed. "Jennie and Gavin. Jennie and Gavin." The kids continued their chant the rest of the way upstairs and into the bedroom where Mom finally hushed them with a no-story-if-you-don't-settle-down threat.

The annoyance was back. Jennie left Gavin standing in the entry. *That was rude, McGrady. He was just trying to be nice.*

She heard him come into the kitchen behind her and ignored him.

"I goofed, didn't I? I'm sorry. I should have asked instead of volunteering our services. I do that sometimes. I mean, if you want I can just leave now—"

"No." Jennie stopped him. "It's okay. I like reading to them. If you left they'd be disappointed."

Gavin offered her a lopsided grin. "Do you want to see the article I wrote about you before or after we read stories?"

Before she could answer, Nick hollered, "Jennie! Gavin! We're ready."

"Jennie and Gabin," Hannah echoed, "we're ready."

Jennie chuckled and shook her head. "I guess that answers your question, Ga-bin, we're being summoned."

In the middle of Gavin's presentation of *The Princess and the Pea*, Hannah fell asleep. Nick held out until the last page of *Little Prince*. Being careful not to wake her, Jennie lifted Hannah from Nick's bed where the four of them had been sitting and placed her in the cot against the wall.

After tucking both of them in and turning out the lights, Jennie led Gavin downstairs, into the kitchen for a Coke, then out to the porch. Jennie sat on the swing and scanned the article Gavin had titled *The New Nancy Drew*. He'd presented her as "an amateur sleuth with a big heart and beautiful cobalt eyes."

"It's too flowery," she said after reading it. "You made me sound too good, too efficient—too everything. You didn't say anything about my being scared spitless—or getting in over my head. Or that I would never have gotten myself kidnapped in the first place if I'd had half a brain."

"You care, Jennie, you're intelligent and decent. . . ."

"I'm obstinate, judgmental, opinionated, and bratty—and I can be extremely rude."

Gavin grinned. "That's true. Can I quote you?"

Jennie punched him in the arm. "I wish I hadn't agreed to let you write this. I really don't want any more publicity."

"Too late," he shrugged. "Already turned it in. I could always write another one."

Jennie punched him again.

For the next hour Gavin told her about his dreams of becoming a television journalist and engaged her in a debate over freedom of the press versus the right to privacy.

The next day at cheerleading tryouts, Jennie found herself arguing again. This time it was with Lisa, who wanted Jennie to try out with her. "Just think of it," Lisa said. "We could go to all the games together."

"I really don't want to be a cheerleader. Besides, I don't know the cheers."

"Yes you do. You helped me learn them. You'd be great."

She'd helped Lisa learn the routines months ago before school let out for the summer. But bouncing around in the backyard was a whole lot different than being in front of the entire school. "Forget it. Look, Lisa, you've got the personality for it, I don't. Now quit bugging me or I'll go call your mom. I'll bet she'd love to know where you are right now."

"You wouldn't." Her eyes widened. For a second, Jennie thought Lisa would hit her, but she backed down. "I just thought it would be fun to do it together, that's all, but if you really don't want to. . . ."

"Don't let her wear you down, McGrady." B.J. thumped Jennie on the shoulder. "Allison's been on my case for a week."

Before Jennie could respond, Gavin climbed up the bleacher seats and dropped down beside her.

A shrill whistle sounded. "Okay everyone, let's get started."

Allison and Lisa bounded down the bleacher steps and hurried toward the voice. A slender woman in a white camp shirt and shorts and a Hawaiian tan stepped onto the field. Short dark hair framed a heart-shaped face.

"Who's that?" Jennie asked.

Gavin answered, "New women's coach and PE teacher.

Name's Diane Dayton. DeeDee for short."

"I thought the school was hurting for money. How could they afford to hire her? The last I heard, the school board was thinking of dropping the athletic program altogether."

"You have been out of touch, haven't you?" Gavin lifted his camera and snapped several photos. "Maybe that's what motivated the guys to work harder. That and Joel's dad." He lowered the camera and looked back at Jennie. "Buck Nielsen is a major contributor to Trinity High and when he talks they listen. Anyway, Nielsen volunteered to come in as an assistant coach last year and really turned things around for all the major sports. We went from being a losing team to being one of the contenders for the league championship."

Joel's father had been a quarterback for one of the top NFL teams a few years ago. After retiring he developed his own line of athletic equipment. "I knew about Joel's dad and getting bumped up in the standings, but how does that translate into more money?"

"More students are enrolling this year, and the sporting events are drawing bigger crowds. I think what topped it off though was the grant Nielsen's company offered. The board decided that with sports generating all that extra money, and Haskell putting so much more energy into coaching the guys, they could hire someone to take over the girls' athletic program."

Gavin raised his camera again. About a dozen girls and two boys gathered around the coach as she blew the whistle again. She separated the girls into groups of threes and fours and told them to begin working through routines.

After their names were called, Lisa, Allison, Courtney, and Annie Koler walked over to their designated space and started stretching. Annie had long straight hair about the same coppery color as Lisa's. She wore it back with no bangs, which seemed to accentuate her oval face and clear, creamy skin. Annie and Lisa could have passed as sisters if Lisa hadn't been so thin and pale.

Another group of girls ran out onto the field, purple and gold pompons waving: Lori Chan, Corky Simmons, Tracy Parouski, and Cassie Nielsen, Joel's sister.

Cassie seemed more the type to play the game than to cheer the teams on. She matched Jennie in height and had the angular build of a weight trainer—the type who'd be good at just about anything.

Tracy and Corky had been on rally squad last year and obviously planned to do it again. Tracy's sun-bleached hair swayed back and forth across her shoulders as she and Corky practiced a yell.

"So who do you think she'll pick?" Gavin asked.

Jennie had no idea. She shifted her attention to Lisa's group. Courtney did a series of backflips, looking like a practiced gymnast.

"Courtney. Definitely." B.J. nodded toward the group. "Allison's looking good too, but Lisa's . . ." B.J. gasped.

Jennie's focus snapped from Courtney to Lisa.

Lisa tossed her brightly-colored pompons into the air and reached out to capture them again. Her knees buckled. She crumpled to the ground. The pompons drifted to earth and settled over her limp body.

7

"I didn't make it, did I?" Lisa stared at the ceiling tiles above her hospital bed. A tear slid from the corner of her eye and trailed into her hair.

Kate soothed back Lisa's matted hair and sighed. "Oh, sweetie, I know how much you wanted this, but . . . no, of course you didn't make it. You shouldn't have even tried."

Lisa took a deep breath and asked, "Who did?"

Their attention shifted to Jennie who was standing beside her aunt.

Jennie avoided Aunt Kate's eyes. She didn't want to see the accusations she knew would be written there. If she had told Aunt Kate about Lisa's plans to go ahead with the cheerleading tryouts, this wouldn't have happened.

"Jennie?" Lisa's voice interrupted Jennie's guilt trip. "Please tell me. Did Allison make it? And Courtney?"

Jennie wouldn't have known the answer if she hadn't just spent the last hour in the hospital cafeteria bringing Allison, B.J., and Gavin up to date on Lisa's condition, which wasn't good.

Jennie stared at the IV tubing, following it to the spot where it entered Lisa's wrist. "They both did—and Annie Koler and Lori Chan." Jennie didn't bother to tell her about the boys—only two had turned out and they were both gymnasts.

Lisa nodded, her lips curling in a weary smile. "They'll make a good team." Lisa closed her eyes and opened them again. "Tracy must be furious. She was really rude to Courtney and Allison during tryouts. I bet that's why DeeDee eliminated her." Lisa's eyes drifted closed again and stayed that way.

"We'd better go," Kate whispered. "We should let her rest for a while." She gave Jennie's shoulder a gentle squeeze and guided her out of the room.

While Aunt Kate made some phone calls, Jennie slumped into a waiting room chair. She'd chosen not to tell Lisa about the fight that had erupted between the girls after DeeDee had made her selection.

According to B.J., Tracy had acted fine until the coach left, then blew up at Courtney, saying the coach had to be color blind to let a girl with purple hair represent the school. B.J., who seemed to enjoy conflicts, had mimicked Tracy saying, "I'm going to be on rally squad this year and I intend to do whatever I have to to change Coach Dayton's mind."

Jennie sniffed and reached into her bag for a tissue. She finally found one, but dug up something else in the search— a white piece of paper. She frowned as she unfolded it, wondering where it had come from. The note had been hand written on a square paper bearing the name, DIANABOL. Jennie suspected it was some sort of drug. The paper had apparently come from a doctor's office—or a pharmacy.

I'm in over my head, the note read. *Call me. Courtney.*

Jennie tried to remember how and when Courtney could have slipped it to her. The last time Jennie had seen the rainbow girl, they'd all been watching the paramedics load Lisa into an ambulance. Courtney had come over to see how Lisa was doing. Then she'd said, "About the phone call, Jennie. . . ."

Before Courtney could finish, Cassie joined them. "You think Lisa's going to be okay?"

"I don't know," Jennie answered.

"You'll keep us posted, won't you?" Cassie seemed genuinely concerned and Jennie promised she'd call later.

"I need to talk to you for a minute," Cassie said as she drew Courtney away from the ambulance. Jennie had watched them walk away, then swung her attention back to Lisa. *How are you going to explain all of this to Aunt Kate, and Mom and Gram?* The question had torpedoed through her mind and exploded in her stomach. She could still feel the effects of it.

Jennie fingered the note from Courtney and forced her attention back to it. She didn't feel like dealing with Courtney Evans at the moment. If it had been anything serious she'd have said something earlier. She tucked the note into her pocket and made plans to call the rainbow girl when she got home.

———————

Jennie couldn't make the call to Courtney until nine that night. After dinner Mom asked her to stay with the kids so she, Gram, and Uncle Kevin could go visit Lisa. Jennie and Kurt, Lisa's eleven-year-old brother, finished feeding Nick and Hannah, gave them baths, and put them to bed. Jennie left Kurt to finish reading *The Little Mermaid* and went up to her room to call Courtney.

Mr. Evans answered. "She's not home. She's gone out with Joel. They were going to pick up Brad and go to the hospital to see Lisa."

Jennie asked him to tell Courtney she'd called. He hesitated for a moment. "Jennie, have you noticed anything strange about Courtney? I mean . . . she's been edgy lately—more so than usual."

Everything about Courtney is strange, Jennie started to say, then stopped. "I don't really know her that well, Mr. Evans. She seemed fine at tryouts today."

He hesitated again, "Is Susan . . . is your mother there by any chance?"

"She's at the hospital too. Want me to have her call you?"

"No, I'll talk with her later. It's just a bookkeeping problem I'm having."

Mom, Gram, and Uncle Kevin arrived as Jennie hung up. She raced up the stairs, nearly colliding with Kurt as he stepped out of Nick's bedroom.

"Your dad's here," she explained and helped him regain his balance.

Even with his thick chestnut hair adding nearly two inches to his height, Kurt barely reached her rib cage. He gazed up into Jennie's eyes, his face round, freckled and healthy looking, like Lisa's used to be. "Do you think Lisa's gonna die?"

His question hit Jennie with the impact of a freight train. "No." Her answer came out more harshly than she had intended. "Why would you think that?"

Kurt shrugged. "'Cause everybody's so sad."

Jennie rested a hand on his shoulder and walked with him down the stairs.

"How's Lisa?" Jennie asked as she and Kurt joined the rest of the family in the kitchen.

"Better," Uncle Kevin said.

"Her blood sugar level and electrolytes are almost back to normal," Mom added as she measured coffee into the filter. "She's been keeping water and apple juice down so it looks like they'll be able to take out the IV in the morning."

Jennie eased into a chair beside Gram, who'd been staring at the table. She glanced up briefly and patted Jennie's hand.

The distant, sad look in Gram's blue eyes shook Jennie. "Are you sure Lisa's going to be okay? You look worried."

"What?" Gram asked, running a hand through her bangs.

"Lisa. Are you sure . . ."

"Oh. No, dear, Lisa's okay, it's . . ." Gram glanced over

at Mom and back at Kevin. "I'm just worried about J.B. He's been called away and—" Gram stopped and shook her head. "Listen to me. Going on like that. I'm getting paranoid in my old age. J.B. is perfectly capable of taking care of himself."

———

Jennie spent a sleepless night worrying. It didn't help that Bernie had chosen her as his designated feeder. Or that she'd forgotten to shut her door all the way again.

At six-thirty, the oversized pup climbed onto her bed, nudging and licking until she got up. Unable to resist his sad brown eyes, Jennie followed him downstairs and fed him. "There," she said, setting the half-empty bag back in the pantry. "I hope you're happy."

Bernie woofed what sounded like a "thank you" and began eating.

She yawned and mumbled, "I'm going back to bed."

Mom stopped her at the foot of the stairs. "I'm glad you're up, honey," she said. "We need to talk."

Jennie groaned in protest, then deciding she probably wouldn't be able to go back to sleep anyway, followed her mother back down the hall and into the kitchen.

After pouring herself a bowl of granola, Jennie reached for the milk. "What did you want to talk to me about? If it's Lisa, I already said I was sorry."

"It's not Lisa. I think you've learned your lesson there." Mom lifted her coffee to her lips and blew on it before taking a tentative sip.

"Then what?"

"How would you feel about my accepting a date with Frank Evans?"

Jennie's mood dropped about twenty degrees. *Lousy.* She shoveled a spoonful of granola and milk into her mouth and chewed on it before answering. Mom's dating Frank presented all sorts of problems Jennie didn't want to think about. Dating could lead to an engagement, which would lead to marriage. Marriage meant having Courtney as a stepsister.

Worse, marriage would eliminate any chance of Mom and Dad getting back together again. "I hate the idea," she finally said.

"Why?" Mom asked. "Is there something you don't like about him, or are you just opposed to my dating anyone?"

Because Dad's still alive. Jennie swallowed back the response and shrugged instead. "I don't think you should jump into anything. I mean, you and Michael just broke up."

"It's only dinner." The toast popped up and Mom pulled out the two slices and buttered them. "I'd like to go. He seems like a nice man."

"Sounds like you've made up your mind, so why ask me?"

Mom slathered strawberry jam on the toast slices and handed one to Jennie. "Believe it or not, I value your opinion. I know we don't always agree, but I do want to know what you think."

"Well . . ." Jennie paused to catch a drip of jam with her tongue. "I told you what I think. Are you going out with him anyway?"

Mom nodded. "Probably." She peered over the rim of her cup and took another drink. "Don't worry. I'm not planning on getting married any time soon."

"Mr. Evans called last night," Jennie said, remembering the phone conversation she'd had with him the night before. "Something about a bookkeeping problem."

"That doesn't surprise me. His records are a mess."

Jennie finished breakfast while she listened to her mother talk about people who dump a year's worth of receipts on her desk and expect her to work miracles. As soon as Jennie could make a break for it, she excused herself and headed upstairs. "I gotta take a shower and get dressed."

"Okay, but don't be too long," Mom called after her. "I'll

need you to take care of the kids for a while this morning while I get some work done."

Jennie took her time showering. The warm water washed away tension as well as soap. On the way back to her room she stopped at the bedroom next to hers and peeked in. Good. Nick and Hannah were still asleep.

Jennie needed some time alone. After getting dressed and braiding her hair, she straightened her room, then pulled a box labeled *Dad's Things* from a closet shelf.

It had been a long time since Jennie had gone through them. The memories assaulted her. She pulled out the tweed hat and scarf, the wooden horse she'd given him as a Christmas gift, and his golf trophy from college, then set them on her bed. She held up the model airplane they'd assembled one winter. Its wings had been broken and hung limply against the plane's side. She'd have to fix it.

Jennie set the plane aside and sorted through the collection of rocks and shells that littered the bottom of the box. Most of the shells lay in pieces. Jennie picked up the shell fragments and after holding them for a long time, threw them away. Some things were too broken to be fixed.

Some things were too broken...

The thought buried itself in her mind. *Too broken to fix.* A light clicked on in Jennie's head. She'd spent a lot of time over the last few years trying to fix things—like her parents' marriage. Maybe their relationship, like the shells she and dad had collected over the years, was too broken. Maybe she needed to let it go, as she'd done with the shells. Let Mom live her life and Dad live his—separately.

Jennie closed her eyes and took a deep breath. She pictured herself standing between Mom and Dad, holding tightly to them, then being split apart as they walked away from each other. If she didn't let go, she'd end up broken too. Jennie imagined herself releasing one, then the other. Tears gathered in her eyes and she hugged herself to lessen the loss.

Jennie kept the picture in her mind while she gathered up her treasures and set them back on the shelf. Maybe she'd leave the airplane too—at least for now. Giggles from the next bedroom told her Nick and Hannah were awake.

A car door slammed from somewhere outside and a minute or so later, the doorbell rang. Maybe it was Aunt Kate with an update on Lisa. Ordinarily she'd have raced down the stairs to answer the door, but decided to let Mom or Nick get it. Jennie didn't feel like talking to anyone just yet.

Before going downstairs, she eyed herself in the mirror. The white shorts and pale pink T-shirt felt as comfortable and cool as they looked. She paused briefly to admire her long tanned legs and suddenly felt guilty. How often had she heard Lisa say, "Jennie, I'm so jealous. You have legs to die for."

She shrugged the guilt aside and turned away from the mirror. *You didn't cause Lisa's illness, McGrady*, she reminded herself. After lunch, when the kids went down for naps, she'd drive over to the hospital to see Lisa.

Before heading downstairs, Jennie placed another call to Courtney. The answering machine picked up. This time Jennie didn't leave a message. Maybe she should add Courtney to the new "Too-Broken-to-Fix" list.

Jennie skipped down the stairs and stopped by the living room to greet Nick and Hannah who were making a "house" out of blankets and sheets. Bernie woofed and shook free of the baby blanket Hannah was trying to wrap around him.

"Bernie, stand still," Hannah ordered. "You s'posed to be the baby."

Feeling sorry for the dog, Jennie suggested an alternate plan. "Why don't you let Bernie play the rescue dog and Hannah's doll can be the baby."

"Okay," they both echoed.

Hearing voices in the kitchen, Jennie headed that way.

"Have you called the police?" Mom asked as Jennie wandered in.

Jennie stopped midstep.

"This morning." Frank Evans was sitting at the table next to Mom. "They think she may have run away."

"Who?" Jennie knew the answer but asked anyway. Instead of joining her mother and Frank at the table, she snagged a barstool and sat at the counter. Somehow it seemed important to keep her distance.

"Courtney's missing," Mom said. "Frank said she didn't come home last night."

8

Jennie was beginning to wonder if her stomach would ever be normal again. Recent events had tied it up in knots the size of basketballs. "Maybe she and Joel decided to do something crazy—drive to the beach, or . . ."

"I called Joel last night around twelve-thirty. He said they'd had an early night. Claims he dropped Courtney off at the house around ten. Brad and Joel's sister Cassie verified Joel's story this morning. I was at the pharmacy until midnight. If she did come home, she must have gone out again. Either that or the kids are lying."

"I doubt that," Jennie jumped to their defense.

"I just can't believe Courtney would run away. We don't always get along—especially since her mother's death, but we have a pretty good relationship." Frank Evans pushed the coffee cup back and forth between his hands. "I've always felt I could trust her."

"She's a teenager, Frank," Mom said as if that was supposed to explain everything. "Even well-adjusted kids," Mom nodded toward Jennie, "—like this one—can have their moments. Maybe Courtney needed to get away for a while."

Jennie didn't know what to say. She could imagine Courtney running away, but not after just having made the rally squad.

"Could you tell if any of her things were missing, an overnight bag, makeup, clothes—that sort of thing?" Jennie asked.

"The police asked me that too. Courtney had enough makeup in her bathroom to start her own cosmetic company. She had so many clothes it's hard to tell. There's a green canvas bag missing, only it's mine. I thought maybe I'd left it at the gym, but I stopped by there this morning and no one had seen it."

Maybe she had run away after all, but why? The phone call and note indicated Courtney was in some kind of trouble. Did that have anything to do with her disappearance? Should she mention the note and phone call to Frank? Yes. The information might provide police with a link. Jennie told Frank what she knew. What she didn't say was that she intended to do some digging of her own.

———

That afternoon at the hospital, one of the knots in Jennie's stomach began to relax. While Lisa still looked like a poster child for a feed-the-hungry campaign, her cheeks were flushed. Sitting up in bed, wearing a bright floral robe with her copper hair up in a pony tail, she seemed almost like the old Lisa again.

"It's about time you got here. Your mom said you left an hour ago."

"Well, ex-cuse me. I thought you might like some flowers." Jennie set the arrangement of pink roses and baby's breath on the bedside stand.

"I'm sorry. They're beautiful. I appreciate the thought, but I've been dying to talk to you about Courtney."

Jennie winced. "Do me a favor, Lisa, and don't use that phrase anymore. I don't want you to *die* for anything."

"Sorry." Lisa wrinkled her nose. "Anyway, tell me what's going on. Have they found her?"

Jennie shook her head. "Not yet. The police are checking

things out. They're pretty sure she ran away." Sinking into a brown vinyl chair, Jennie related her conversation with Frank Evans that morning then asked, "So what do you think? Did she run?"

"I suppose it's possible. When she was here last night with Brad and Joel, she seemed . . . I don't know, distant and scared, maybe. She's a hard person to read. When I asked her about cheerleading, she shrugged it off—like she didn't really care."

Jennie told her about the note Courtney had slipped into her bag at tryouts. "Did she say anything yesterday while you were practicing?"

Lisa fingered the folds of her robe. "I can't think of anything. Except . . ." Her green eyes locked with Jennie's.

"What?"

"Last night just before they left she said she needed to go home early. She had some business to take care of."

"Business? Like packing?"

"I have no idea. Maybe we should talk to Cassie and Joel. She might have said something to them."

"We?" Jennie raised an eyebrow and gave Lisa an incredulous look. "Mom said you had to be in here for another day, at least."

"Don't remind me," she pouted. "Anyway, she could have confided in them."

"I thought I'd talk to them tonight at the youth meeting." About once a month they'd head down to Pioneer Square or Waterfront Park and hand out tracts—fact sheets about drugs, sex, and AIDS. Some of the more talented kids—musicians, singers, and dancers—performed and gave their testimonies. Michael had started the practice saying he wanted to reach some of Portland's homeless kids—not to preach at them, but to educate them and let them know someone cared. Jennie planned to use the opportunity to question some of the kids in the youth group about Courtney.

Lisa sighed. Her eyes drifted closed. "I wish I could go," she murmured.

"So do I," Jennie whispered. She watched her cousin for a few moments. When Lisa didn't open her eyes again, Jennie left.

On the way home, Jennie stopped at the church to talk to Michael. She wasn't sure why. Well, that wasn't quite true. About two seconds after the secretary buzzed him to let him know Jennie was there, his office door swung open. "Jennie! Come in." He stepped aside to let her in, then closed the door behind him. "Have a seat." He pointed to two blue-and-white upholstered chairs and folded himself into the one closest to him. Jennie sank into the other.

She glanced around the office. At least two hundred books with titles like *Hermeneutics, Biblical Archeology*, and *Church History* lined one wall. Her gaze lingered on a metal sculpture of the crucifix sitting on his desk.

"Like it?"

Jennie nodded.

"It's a bronze. Picked it up in Jerusalem a few years ago. The first piece in the Rhode's Gallery art collection." Michael laughed. "Actually it's the only piece so far." He hesitated, his smile faded. "But you didn't come to learn about fine arts did you? Everything okay at home?"

Jennie dragged her eyes from the statue to Michael's face. "I guess. Except for Lisa." Jennie sighed. "Did you know Mom was thinking about dating Frank Evans?"

Michael cleared his throat and looked down at his clasped hands. "Yes. As a matter of fact, I introduced them."

"How could you do that? I thought you loved Mom."

"Jennie . . ." he ran a hand through his sandy brown hair. His blue gaze met hers. "I do, but I just don't think it's ever going to work between us. Your mother wants someone more . . . I don't know. I'm devoted to my work—to the youth group. If she can't accept who I am . . ." He shrugged and lifted his hands in a what-can-I-do? gesture.

Jennie ran her fingers along the chair's seam. "This is stupid. I shouldn't have come."

"It's not stupid. I'm glad you're here. Like I said before, my door is always open to you." Michael stood and walked over to his desk. "In fact, I was going to call you. You know about Courtney being missing?"

Jennie nodded. "Yeah. Why?"

"I made some of these up today." He handed her a flyer. "I knew you'd want to help and thought this might be a good place to start."

The word MISSING marched across the top of the page in bold black letters. Under it was a picture of Courtney along with her age and a description. "They're offering a reward?"

"The police thought we'd have a better chance of getting information. I was hoping you and some of the kids from the youth group would help me distribute them when we do our street ministry tonight."

"You think she might be downtown?"

"Maybe. She seemed to enjoy going down there and talking to the homeless kids. Courtney has a real gift for helping people. Through her intervention we've been able to get three kids off the street and into programs where they'll get the help they need. If she did run away, my guess is that she'd go there."

Jennie agreed. They spent the next hour talking. Actually Jennie talked while Michael mostly listened. When she left, nothing had really changed—except maybe her anxiety level.

———

That evening as they boarded the Trinity Center bus, Jennie got her opportunity to talk to Brad, Joel, and Cassie all at the same time. The guys had taken separate seats, one behind the other. Cassie slipped into the seat next to Brad, which Jennie might have found disconcerting if they hadn't both asked about Lisa. She hoped Brad and Cassie didn't have something going. It would really tear Lisa up if he broke up with her now.

"She looked much better today," Jennie stopped in the aisle to talk to them. "I'm still worried about her."

"I wanted to go by and see her this afternoon," Brad said, stretching his arms out in front of him. The muscles in his shoulders bulged under his black T-shirt. "But the coach kept us over. We barely had time to get cleaned up and eat."

Now that Jennie thought about it, maybe Cassie was more Brad's type than Lisa. She was taller, sturdier. In fact, seeing Brad, Cassie, and Joel together sent a wave of empathy through her. No wonder Lisa felt so insecure. The three of them looked like perfect candidates for the cover of *Sports Illustrated.*

Joel's somber expression gave way to a smile as Jennie took the space beside him. "Hey, if it isn't our very own super sleuth." He shifted his bulky shoulders and extended a muscular arm across the seat behind her. His sleeveless T-shirt stretched across a chest that would have made Arnold Schwarzenegger proud. "So what do you want to know?"

"Excuse me?" Jennie felt like a kid with her hand caught in a cookie jar. Was she that transparent?

"About Courtney. You're on the case, right? You're going to try to find out what happened to her."

Jennie shrugged. "Well," she admitted, "I am curious. But I'm not on the case."

"Come on, Jennie, be honest." Cassie twisted around in her seat so she could face Jennie and her brother. "You think we'll tell you something we didn't tell the police." She glanced at Joel then back at Jennie. "I really wish we had some answers. Truth is, Joel and Brad picked me up at the mall at nine. We stopped at Wendy's for a snack and dropped

Courtney off at about ten. After that, we took Brad to his place and went home."

"The police think she ran away," Jennie said. "Personally, I have a hard time with that, but then, I don't know her all that well. Did she say anything to you?"

"Yeah, she did." Joel huffed disgustedly and fingered the rim of his Miami Dolphins baseball cap. He shook his head. "I'm surprised she didn't take off sooner."

"Why?" Jennie asked.

"Ask her father." Joel folded his arms and stared out the window.

"According to him they get along fairly well," Jennie countered, bracing herself as the bus turned a corner.

"He's lying." Cassie pursed her lips as though deliberating whether or not to go on. After a moment she did. "They fight all the time. He hit her really hard the other day. Here." Cassie pointed at her front left shoulder. "She showed me the bruise."

"Mr. Evans?" Somehow, Jennie didn't see him as an abusive parent, but then you couldn't always tell. She'd long since learned that appearances could be deceiving. *If he really is abusive, McGrady, that puts a whole new light on things. Maybe Courtney called to ask for help—or to warn me and Mom. Maybe Frank beat Courtney up and has her hidden somewhere . . . .* "Did you tell the police?"

"What good would that do?" Joel asked. "Evans would just deny it. Who are the police going to believe? A couple of kids or some rich dude pharmacist? Besides, she's safe now."

"How do you know she's safe?" Jennie asked. "Did she tell you where she was going?"

Joel didn't answer.

"Come on you guys, are you hiding her somewhere?"

Cassie looked Jennie square in the eyes. "No. I wish we were. We're as worried about Courtney as you are. It's just that if she ran away and if she's on the streets, she's probably okay."

"Cassie's right." Joel unfolded his arms and turned toward her, then rested his arm on the seat back again. "She asked me to come downtown with her a couple of times. I don't know, maybe it was her hair or the way she dressed, but the kids seemed to like her. So I figure if she's with them—they'll watch out for her, you know?"

The three athletes managed to shift the conversation from Courtney to sports. Jennie's mind stuck to Frank Evans and his missing daughter. At least now she wouldn't have to worry about Mom dating him. She'd have to warn Mom before . . .

The bus made a sharp turn, throwing Jennie against Joel and scattering her thoughts. His chest was rock hard against her shoulder. "Sorry," she stammered. "The turn caught me by surprise."

When Jennie tried to straighten, Joel held her in place. "Me too," he murmured. "But, hey, I'm not complaining."

His breath fluttered against her cheek like butterfly wings. Her stomach tightened. For a moment Jennie found herself wondering what it would be like to kiss him. But only for a moment. Startled at her response, she jerked back. He let her go, but not before giving her a conceited I-know-you-want-me smile.

"Cool your jets, Nielsen," Jennie muttered.

Joel wasn't her type. He was too—too bulky. And he was Courtney's boyfriend.

Wait a minute. Jennie backed up her brain and replayed the incident. *Something doesn't compute here, McGrady. Joel's girlfriend has been missing for what? Twenty-four hours? And he's making a pass at you? Either Joel knows more than he's letting on or he's a total jerk.*

Since they all seemed genuinely concerned about Courtney's disappearance, Jennie went with her second impression.

Before heading out to distribute flyers and fact sheets on drugs and AIDS, Michael gave them some last-minute instructions, which, as always, included the buddy system. They were to go out in groups of twos, threes and fours, but never alone. Instructions complete, the kids started drifting off.

Ordinarily Jennie would have paired up with Lisa. She looked around for B.J. and Allison, then remembered they'd gone to the beach with their parents. She thought about teaming up with Joel, Cassie, and Brad, but didn't see them.

Jennie was beginning to feel like the last person picked for a baseball team when Gavin tapped her on the shoulder. "Will I do?"

"Perfectly." The word slipped out before Jennie could stop it. The last thing she wanted to do was encourage him.

Gavin turned out to be a great partner. Having dated Courtney he knew her favorite haunts and remembered meeting some of the kids she'd befriended.

They didn't find Courtney, but they did talk to a dozen kids who recognized her picture and two people who had seen her the night before. Randy, a student at Portland State who worked at The Eatery, recognized Courtney's picture immediately.

"Wow," he said, "I can't believe she's missing." He reached up to shove back a straw-colored swatch of hair. "If I tell you what I know do I get the two hundred?"

"If you call the number on the flyer and if they find her, you might," Jennie answered.

"So why should I tell you anything?"

"Because I think she might be in trouble and I want to help."

He shrugged. "Courtney comes in once or twice a week. She came in last night around eleven."

"Last night? You're sure?" Jennie asked, trying to concentrate on why she was there, rather than why he'd shave his head and leave a tail hanging in his face.

"Yeah. I remember 'cause she seemed different, you know? Like nervous, maybe, or scared. She kept looking at the door like maybe she was waiting for someone."

"And did this person ever show?"

"I don't think so. The only one I saw her talking to was Tina."

They were getting close. Jennie's heart did a triple flip. "Tina," Jennie repeated. "Do you know her last name?"

"Nope. Just Tina."

"Any idea where I can find her?"

"Yep." He nodded toward the door. "She just walked in."

9

"Hey, Tina," Randy called to the girl with burgundy hair who was backing into the restaurant. "How's it goin'?"

"Been better." Favoring a bandaged right foot, Tina turned, then crutch-walked across the room and settled her small frame into a bench seat in the far corner near the window. She placed the crutches on the floor beside her and started to remove her studded black leather jacket. A bright yellow knit tank top contrasted sharply with her mahogany skin.

She eyed Jennie and Gavin wearily and shrugged the jacket back on again. Tina reminded Jennie of a little girl wearing dress-up clothes several sizes too big. Jennie remembered seeing the jacket—or one like it—on Courtney.

Randy grabbed a hamburger and box of fries from the warmer and set them on a tray along with a salad and a carton of milk, then delivered them to Tina's table. Not only routine, but gratis, Jennie noticed. He leaned on the table and nodded his head toward Jennie and Gavin. "Couple kids here asking about Courtney Evans."

Tina muttered something unintelligible and grabbed for her crutches. Her dark eyes flashed angrily at Randy.

"Wait!" Jennie hurried to the table. "Please. We're Courtney's friends. She's missing and . . ." Jennie handed Tina a flyer. "We just want to make sure she's safe."

"Don't know nuthin' about it," Tina insisted. She glanced briefly at Courtney's picture, pulled a French fry out of the box and shoved it into her mouth.

Gavin slid into the bench opposite Tina and made room for Jennie to sit beside him.

"Hey, don't I know you?" Tina asked, scooping up another fry.

Gavin nodded. "We met a couple months ago. Courtney introduced us."

"Oh yeah. The guy with the camera. You're not gonna try takin' my picture again, are you?"

"And have you ruin another roll of film? No way."

Tina chuckled and glanced toward Jennie. "Who's she?"

Gavin introduced Jennie as a friend of his and Courtney's.

Tina peeled off the wrapper of her hamburger. "Hope you guys don't mind if I eat in front of you. Low blood sugar, you know."

Jennie watched her eat, wondering how best to phrase her questions. "Um . . . Tina," Jennie hesitated. "About Courtney. She didn't come home last night and . . ."

"Like I said, I don't know nuthin'."

"But you saw her last night."

"Yeah." Tina paused to swallow. "She comes around—oh, 'bout once a week or so. Sees how I'm doing. Talks to some of the other kids. Courtney's a good person. Always helpin' people."

Jennie tried another approach. "Randy said she seemed different last night—scared, maybe. Do you know where she was going after you talked to her—or if she was meeting anyone?"

"Nope. We left at the same time. I went one way, she went the other."

Several questions later, Jennie realized she'd gotten all the information Tina intended to give. She thanked her and

Randy and left several flyers. On the back of the one she'd given Tina, Jennie wrote her name and phone number. "If you see Courtney, have her call me."

Tina didn't answer.

Out on the sidewalk Jennie heaved a long, exasperated sigh. It was nine o'clock—time to head back to the bus. "I wish I'd driven my car. I have a feeling Tina knows more than she's telling us. I'd love to wait around and follow her."

Gavin shook his head. "Wouldn't work. She's too smart for that. If she does know where Courtney is, she'll tell her we're looking for her. Courtney will either call us or not."

"I suppose you're right."

"Come on." Gavin draped an arm across her shoulders. "We'd better get back."

Jennie thought about pulling away from him, but didn't. Unlike Joel, Gavin's gesture carried no sexual overtones, only friendship. "So," Jennie said as she fell into step beside him, "tell me about Tina and how she managed to ruin your film."

"The first time Courtney brought me down here with her, I started taking photos like crazy. Thought I might do an article on homeless kids. Most of them didn't mind, but Tina went wild. Told me if I didn't give her the film, she was going to smash my camera."

"That's pretty tough talk for someone so little."

"Tina's tougher than she looks. Besides, she had some big friends and I wasn't about to tangle with those dudes. One word from her and they'd have smashed the camera *and* my head."

"Why so camera shy?"

"She's a runaway. Courtney said she is only thirteen. Her parents are alcoholics. She's been in a dozen foster homes since she was five and a few months ago decided she'd be better off living on the streets."

"That's so sad."

"Yeah. But you hang out here long enough and you hear

73

all kinds of stories like that. Courtney wanted to help them all." Gavin frowned and stuffed his hands in his pockets.

Before boarding the bus, they pooled the information they'd learned about Courtney. A few of the others had talked to kids who recognized her, but no one admitted to knowing where she was or whether or not she'd run away. Gavin didn't mention Tina so Jennie didn't either. If the police started asking questions, Tina might get scared off.

Michael commended them. "We'll give this to the police and hope they're able to come up with some answers."

Jennie arrived back at the house around ten. Frank's Lexus was parked in the driveway. She sat in the Mustang for a few minutes gathering her thoughts. Joel and the others had made some frightening accusations against Courtney's father. Jennie wished she had the nerve to walk in and ask him whether or not they were true.

Mr. Evans, she imagined herself saying, *my sources tell me you beat up your daughter*. Right. He'd just deny it and Mom would come unglued. No, she'd have to engage in as normal a conversation as she could and try to read between the lines. Later she'd tell Mom what she'd learned.

Jennie exited the car and strolled up the walk, wondering how best to make her entrance. At the door, she took a deep breath to steel herself—against what, Jennie wasn't sure.

As Jennie opened the door, she heard voices coming from the living room.

"I wish I knew what to do," Frank was saying. "Courtney's never run away before."

Jennie quietly closed the door and tiptoed across the entry floor. Okay, so eavesdropping wasn't the most ethical way to get information, but it could be effective.

Frank and Mom were sitting together on the sofa with their backs to Jennie. "What am I doing wrong, Susan?" Frank asked. "What did I do to drive her away?"

Jennie pinched her lips together. *Knocking her around might have done it.*

"Don't be so hard on yourself," Mom said, leaning toward him. The couch hid all but their heads and shoulders, but knowing her mom, Jennie suspected she'd taken hold of his hand. "It may not have anything to do with you. Not long ago, Jennie ran away. She was going through a hard time accepting her father's death and went to the coast to visit her grandmother."

Enough. Talking about Courtney was one thing, but Jennie did not want her mother telling Frank stories about her. Jennie stepped back into the entry, opened the door and closed it again. "Mom," she said, announcing her arrival, "I'm back."

She walked into the living room, leaned over the couch, and kissed her mother's cheek.

"Hi, sweetheart. How was the meeting?"

"Good." As Jennie told them about their search, she watched Frank's face. "We handed out a lot of flyers. Gavin and I talked to a couple of people who saw Courtney last night."

Frank frowned and shook his head. "God only knows what terrible things could happen to her down there. I kept asking her not to go. She just wouldn't listen. I . . ." He closed his eyes and took a deep breath. "I'll never forgive myself if anything happens to her."

Jennie couldn't tell. She honestly couldn't tell whether or not Frank Evans was sincere. He seemed broken up about Courtney's disappearance, but that didn't indicate whether or not he had been the reason for her running away.

Frank left a few minutes later. While Mom walked him outside, Jennie filled two cups with water and set them in the microwave. She'd just put them on the table and dropped in the peppermint tea bags when Mom came back inside.

"Tea!" Mom crossed the kitchen and gave Jennie a hug. "That's so sweet."

Jennie shrugged. "Thought maybe you could use it. Besides, I wanted to talk to you about something." She waited until her mother had removed the tea bag and taken a sip, then told her about the bruises Cassie had seen on Courtney. "He hits her, Mom. That's why she ran away."

Mom stared at the greenish brown liquid. "I don't know what to say. Frank is one of the nicest men I've ever met. I . . ." Mom shifted her gaze from the cup to Jennie's face. "Honey, could your friends have made a mistake?"

"Courtney told them she was afraid of her dad. Cassie saw the bruises."

Mom sighed. "If it's true, we should tell the police. But . . ." She stopped, her brows furrowed in thought. "I'll talk to Michael first."

Jennie placed a hand on her mother's arm. "I'm sorry, Mom. I really am."

Her mother nodded and stared into her tea again. After a few minutes of silence, Jennie moved quietly away from the table, dumped her remaining tea in the sink, and left the room.

The phone in her room rang as Jennie pulled a light cotton nightshirt over her head. Two rings later she'd managed to work her arms out of the sleeve holes so she could answer it.

"Jennie," a raspy voice whispered.

Jennie stopped breathing. "Who. . . ?"

"It's me—Courtney."

10

"Where are you?" Jennie's heart leapt into high gear.

"Never mind that." Courtney coughed. Apparently she had a cold.

"Are you all right?" Jennie asked.

"Yes."

"Why did you run away? Everyone's been worried about you."

"Can't talk here. I need to see you."

"When?"

"Now."

Jennie hesitated. "I don't know."

"Please. I have to talk to someone. You're the only one I can trust."

"Courtney, if it's about your father . . ."

"No. Whatever you do, don't say anything to him. Just meet me in South Park Blocks by the statue of Teddy Roosevelt."

Jennie weighed the options. *If you refuse, Courtney might end up in terrible trouble. If you go, you might be able to talk her into getting help.* Courtney wouldn't have to go back home.

"Okay," Jennie said finally. "But look for my car—a red Mustang. I'll drive by and pick you up. We'll go somewhere safe and talk."

Courtney agreed.

Jennie changed back into jeans and a sweatshirt. The dark hallway and narrow strip of light under her mother's bedroom door told her that Mom had gone to bed. Jennie sneaked downstairs, out the door, and into the night.

Shifting the car into neutral, she let it back out of the driveway before starting the engine. *You shouldn't be doing this, McGrady. Mom's going to kill you.* "Hopefully," Jennie mumbled, "she won't find out."

A block away, Jennie almost went back to talk to Mom, or at least write a note, then decided against it. She wanted to get to Courtney as quickly as possible.

With her windows up and the car doors locked, Jennie drove around the Park Blocks four times. On the fifth time around, Jennie stopped the car near the Roosevelt Rough Rider statue and looked into the park's shadowy depths.

"Where are you, Courtney?" Jennie asked aloud. She didn't want to give up, but had no intention of getting out of the car to look for her.

Jennie was about to drive on when headlights glared behind her. She gripped the steering wheel, then relaxed her hands when she caught a glimpse of the uniform. A police officer tapped on her window. Jennie groped for the power button to lower the window and finally found it.

The officer, a woman, lifted her flashlight, shining it in Jennie's face and into the car. "I'd like to see your driver's license, please."

"I was supposed to meet a friend down here," Jennie explained as she reached into the bag on the passenger seat and withdrew her wallet. She fished out the license and handed it to the officer.

When she directed the flashlight beam to the driver's license, Jennie could barely make out the name badge— Sgt. R.L. Brown.

Officer Brown went back to the patrol car and after a few

minutes returned. "So you're the McGrady girl. I've heard about you."

"Oh." From the flat tone of her voice, Jennie couldn't tell if that was good or bad.

"Out kind of late, aren't you?"

Jennie explained again. This time she handed the officer one of the flyers she and the others had distributed earlier that night. "Courtney asked me to meet her here. I'm worried something might have happened to her."

Officer Brown scanned the flyer. "What time did she call you?"

"Around eleven," Jennie said. "She insisted I meet her alone. I told her I'd pick her up. Didn't want to walk around in the park by myself."

Brown nodded. "Good move. Staying home and calling us would have been even better."

"I thought I could help. I don't understand why she's not here."

"She may have seen the patrol car and gotten cold feet."

Brown's explanation seemed plausible, but Jennie had a sick feeling in the pit of her stomach. Her intuition told her it wasn't that simple. Courtney had asked for help three different times. "Could you help me check out the area in case . . . I mean, someone might have attacked her or something before I got here."

Brown looked at the poster again and back at Jennie. "I'll call for backup. In the meantime I'd like you to go on home."

"Can't I go with you? She called me and . . ."

"Miss McGrady." The sergeant put her hands on her hips. "Either go home now, or I'll haul you in for breaking curfew."

"Okay. I'm going, but could you call me if you find her? I'd like to know."

Officer Brown's look of disapproval softened. "I'll think about it."

Jennie scribbled her phone number on the flyer and left.

———————

When Jennie pulled into the driveway, the lights were on all over the house. That meant Mom had gotten up again. Great. *Take it easy, McGrady*, Jennie told herself. *Maybe she doesn't know you went out. Maybe you can sneak in and...*

The front door snapped open as Jennie stepped onto the porch. Mom stood in the entry, her hair as wild as the look on her face. "Where have you been?"

"Courtney called," Jennie explained, hoping to defuse her mother before the explosion came. "She asked me to meet her downtown."

It worked. Sort of. Mom closed her eyes the way she did when she counted to ten to keep from losing her temper. She waited for Jennie to come in, then closed the door.

"And you went—just like that? Couldn't you have at least told me?"

"She asked me not to." Jennie sank onto the living room couch.

"Where is she?" Mom raked her fingers through her hair, trying to restore some kind of order to her curls and probably the situation.

Jennie shrugged. "I don't know. She never showed up. I gave the information to the police and came home." Mom was not impressed.

"You shouldn't have gone alone."

"But, Mom, I had no choice."

Mom tossed her a why-did-I-ever-have-children look. "Go to bed, Jennie. It's late and I'm far too angry to discuss this rationally."

This time Jennie didn't argue.

The next morning Jennie's private phone rang at seven in the morning. "H'lo," she murmured into the receiver.

"Miss McGrady?" Jennie didn't recognize the woman's

voice. "This is Sergeant Brown—Portland police. You wanted me to call if we learned anything about Courtney Evans."

"You found her?"

Brown hesitated. "Yes, but not in the park. A sanitation crew found her in a dumpster around five this morning."

11

"A dumpster?" Jennie repeated the words she couldn't possibly have heard. "Is Courtney dead?"

"Not quite, but from the beating she took, it looks like someone wanted her that way." The officer's businesslike voice belied the horror of the words she'd spoken.

"I can't believe it."

"Any idea who might have wanted this kid dead?"

Her father. Jennie wanted to say the words but they got stuck in her throat. Fathers didn't beat up their kids and throw them away. *Some did,* a voice reminded her, but Jennie didn't want to listen to that one. Instead, she grasped another, more acceptable thought. Courtney had been the victim of a mugging.

Jennie took a couple of deep breaths to steady herself.

"Jennie?" Brown's voice penetrated her thoughts. "You still with me?"

"Y-yes," Jennie stammered. "I just can't believe it. Are you sure it was Courtney?"

"'Fraid so. She didn't have any ID on her, but you'd given me the poster. I contacted her father. He met me at the hospital and gave us a positive identification."

"Is—is she going to be okay?" Jennie asked.

Brown hesitated. "It doesn't look good. She's in a coma. We'll know more after we get a report from the doctors."

Oh, God, Jennie prayed. *Please let her be okay. Don't let her die.*

"We'll need you to come down to the station sometime today to give us a statement," Brown went on. "Looks like you may have been one of the last ones to talk to her before she was attacked."

"Um—sure." Even though she already knew, Jennie listened to Brown's instructions regarding the location of the police station and what to do when she got there.

Still dazed, she walked over to her window and folded herself onto the deep cushions. Jennie shook her head. *How could something like this happen?* Kids she knew didn't get beaten up and thrown into dumpsters. That only happened to thugs in the movies—didn't it? Only hours ago, Courtney had asked for help. What kind of trouble had she gotten into? Could it have been a random mugging? At least a dozen questions flooded Jennie's mind. Questions she intended to find answers to. She owed Courtney that much.

A gentle knock on the door interrupted Jennie's jumbled thoughts, bringing a rush of relief. She hurried to unlock the door.

"Frank just called." Mom pinched her lips together, then released them. "Courtney's in the hospital."

"I know. The police just told me."

Mom frowned. "I don't understand. Why would the police call you?" She hesitated a moment. "Does this have anything to do with your being gone last night?"

Jennie nodded, and explained the events of the night before. "I had to go, Mom. She sounded so scared."

"You should have talked to me first—and the police. You shouldn't have gone alone. Jennie, it could just as easily have been you lying in that hospital bed."

"I didn't get out of the car," Jennie began in her own defense. "I had the doors locked."

"You broke curfew."

"Mom. . . ."

"Stop. I don't want to argue with you. I know you thought you were making the right choice, but . . ." She paused to take another deep breath. "I'm going to get dressed and go to the hospital. Frank needs my support right now."

He's probably the one who put her there. Courtney's the one who needs us, Jennie wanted to argue, but didn't. "I'd like to go see her, too."

Mom hesitated. "Maybe Kate or Gram can watch Nick."

"I'll call Gram," Jennie said, feeling the need to touch base with her. Having been on the police force for ten years, Gram might have some insights.

"I'm so sorry about your friend, Jennie," Gram said after hearing Jennie's story.

"I don't want to believe that Mr. Evans did it, but after what Joel and Cassie said . . ." Jennie hesitated, hoping Gram would have some answers.

"Abuse is a possibility the police will want to pursue—especially if she's a runaway." Gram's voice, even on the phone, had a stabilizing effect on Jennie. "You said you were going down to the station this afternoon to make a statement. Would you like me to come with you?"

"Would you?" Jennie felt like a boulder had fallen from her shoulders. Until that moment, Jennie hadn't realized how much she was dreading her encounter with the police. "Oh, Gram, thank you." She almost said goodbye when she remembered her reason for calling. Gram agreed to take care of Nick and Hannah and promised to be there within the hour.

"I'll tell you what, dear," Gram said before hanging up. "It's been a long time since you and I have had time to ourselves. If it's all right with your mother, why don't the two of us have a nice lunch when you get back from the hospital? We'll do that before we go to the police department. It will give us a chance to catch up."

When Jennie and her mom arrived at the hospital, they found Frank Evans pacing across the floor of a large waiting room situated outside the hospital's surgical unit. His bowed shoulders lifted some as Mom walked toward him. He stretched out his arms and embraced her.

Jennie stared at them. Hadn't Mom believed her? Jennie wanted to scream at her, *He's the enemy. He's the one who hit Courtney.*

Frank held Mom for a moment, then fastened his gaze on Jennie. "Thanks for coming."

Jennie unclenched her fists, but didn't respond.

"How is she?" Mom asked. "They told us at the front desk that she was in surgery."

"I don't know. The doctor said he needed to remove a blood clot to relieve pressure on her brain. She has a collapsed lung and . . ." He shook his head and moved his right hand up to cover his eyes. "There's so much. She's been in there for over an hour already."

Mom reached up and touched his shoulders. "Why don't we sit down." To Jennie she said, "Can you get us some coffee, hon? I think we could both use a cup."

Jennie set her bag on the seat next to Mom and tried to push her anger aside. She walked slowly in the direction of the coffee maker on the opposite side of the room. Watching Frank twisted her insides into massive knots. Somehow he wasn't acting like a guy who'd nearly beaten his own daughter to death, but then what did she know? It wasn't as if she saw people like that everyday. He could be acting, she reminded herself. Some people were good at that.

Jennie watched Frank closely as she handed him and Mom their coffee in Styrofoam cups. His blue gaze met hers briefly as he murmured "thank you," then looked away. She took the chair opposite Frank, but after five minutes of watching him stare into his coffee cup, decided her intuition had gone on vacation.

Jennie needed something to do. Why couldn't Lisa have been in this hospital instead of the one in east county? At least then she could have visited her while they were waiting. "I can't handle sitting around like this," Jennie finally said, bouncing to her feet. "I'm going down to the cafeteria for a Coke."

Mom nodded and turned her attention back to Frank.

Twenty-five minutes later, with a blueberry bagel, cream cheese, and a soft drink still churning in her stomach, Jennie decided to head back to the surgical waiting area. Not wanting to wait for an elevator, she took the stairs.

The echo in the stairwell reminded Jennie of another stairwell in another hospital—and the terror she'd felt when cornered in a similar space by a murderer. Her heart pounded as she placed one foot in front of the other. *He'd been a nice guy too*, Jennie mused. *Nice and deadly.*

The incident had affected her more than she'd thought. She turned around, intending to go back to the elevator, then stopped. *Come on, McGrady, you are not going to let one bad incident give you panic attacks for the rest of your life. Just keep moving.*

Jennie raced up the first two floors, slowing only when her lungs and legs threatened to collapse if she didn't stop abusing them. By the time she reached the third floor her breathing had almost returned to normal. *See*, she told herself. *There's nothing to be afraid of. It's not going to happen again so just relax.*

A door opened overhead. Panic exploded in her chest. Laughter filled the empty spaces around her as two women in white uniforms came into view. They smiled as they passed, then resumed their conversation. Jennie gripped the railing, took a deep breath, and kept moving. *You're going to make it, McGrady. Only one more floor.* When she reached the fourth floor, Jennie flung open the door and stepped into the lobby.

She was still puffing when she reached the waiting room. Mom sat there alone, reading a magazine. "Where's Frank?" Jennie asked as she sat down next to her.

"Talking to the police."

"Are they going to arrest him?"

Obviously irritated, Mom closed the magazine and tossed it on a coffee table. "Jennie, I know you think Frank is responsible for this, but I don't believe it for a minute. He's devastated by what's happened. I don't know why Courtney told her friends that her dad hit her, but she must have been lying."

"Why would she do that?"

"The police told us they had found Valium in her pockets and traces of amphetamines in her blood. They think she may have gotten them from her father's pharmacy."

"Drugs? Courtney was doing drugs?"

12

Drugs.

There's your motive, McGrady. Courtney was helping herself to drugs and good old dad found out about it. Maybe he confronted her, they fought. The rest is history.

Jennie was about to relate all this to her mother when Frank returned. Michael walked in with him.

Frank looked dazed and, once again, Jennie felt sorry for him. "I don't understand any of this," he said, his gaze darting from one to the other. "Courtney didn't take drugs—I'm certain of it. She knows how dangerous they are."

"But we did find a discrepancy in your books, Frank," Mom said. "You said yourself that some of your inventory is missing."

"Yes, but not the controlled drugs." He sat down, resting his elbows on his knees. "If Courtney was on drugs, I would have known."

"Not necessarily." Michael gripped Frank's shoulder. "It's sad, but parents are often the last to know."

"But I'm a pharmacist. . . ."

"Mr. Evans?" The deep male voice came from a man in green surgical scrubs.

Frank raised his head, and placing his hands against his knees, pushed himself into a standing position. "Courtney, is she. . . ?"

"She made it through surgery. We'll be transferring her to Intensive Care shortly."

"Can I see her?"

"Not for a couple of hours. Why don't you have something to eat and we'll page you."

Frank nodded and turned to Michael. "Can you stay?"

"Sorry, I have an appointment at the church."

Jennie, definitely not wanting to hang around with her mother and Frank for the next two hours, asked Michael to drop her off at the house. "I need to go to the police station this afternoon," she added for emphasis.

"Sure." Michael glanced at Mom. "That is, if it's okay with your mother."

"Fine. Jennie, tell Gram I'll be home sometime this afternoon. I'd like to stay with Frank until Courtney's stable."

So much for having lunch with Gram.

Jennie and Michael said goodbye and left. Once in the parking lot, Michael led her to his BMW and unlocked the door. "Want to drive?"

"Sure." Jennie grinned and wedged herself into the driver's seat. Sheer luxury. Sitting behind the wheel of the sports car drained the tension from her neck and shoulders.

Once she'd merged onto the freeway, Jennie chanced a look at Michael. He stared straight ahead, seemingly deep in thought.

"What are you thinking about?" she asked.

He sighed and shook his head. "Just trying to make some sense of this thing. Courtney's a good kid. I know she comes off as tough and rebellious at times, but that's all an act. I have to admit, I find the drug thing hard to imagine. Why anyone would want to beat her up like that—"

"I think it was her dad," Jennie said, relaying the conversation she'd had with Joel and Cassie.

"They told me that too. Came in yesterday afternoon. Apparently Courtney had told them not to say anything. She didn't want to get her dad in trouble. Cassie and Joel decided they'd better tell someone. They were worried that Frank might have done something to her. If fact, that's what initiated the search. I'm not sure I buy it though."

"Why?" Jennie tried unsuccessfully to keep the irritation out of her voice.

"Courtney and her dad had their differences—all families do, but somehow I just don't see him as an abuser."

"So you think Courtney lied?" Jennie set her jaw, anger rising inside her like a geyser. "What if she didn't? What if her dad is the one who's lying?" Jennie paused in her tirade to pass an extremely slow van.

Seeing she had his attention, she went on. "Why is it so hard for adults to believe kids? It just isn't fair."

"Jennie, calm down. And while you're at it, you might want to let up on the gas pedal just a tad. I think the speed limit along here is fifty."

Jennie glanced at the speedometer and winced. Seventy-five? "Sorry." She slowed down and glanced in the rearview mirror, half expecting to see a bank of flashing lights bearing down on her.

"You're safe," Michael said. "This time."

"I really am sorry. But I meant what I said."

"I know. You've brought up some good points. I'm not accusing anyone of lying. Basically, I'm just trying to make sense of it all."

"Me too."

They didn't talk much the rest of the way. Jennie mainly concentrated on maintaining an acceptable speed limit. She took the exit off the freeway and angled down the streets leading toward the Crystal Lake area and home.

They'd no sooner pulled into the driveway when Nick and Bernie came bounding down the porch steps. Before Michael could even get out of the car, Nick had him in a head lock.

"Whoa. Take it easy, big fella." Michael laughed and extricated himself from the car, then swung Nick into his arms and onto his shoulders. Jennie blinked back the tears that always seemed to threaten when she saw Nick and Michael together. How could Mom be so blind? Couldn't she see? Michael was perfect for Nick. Almost as perfect as their real dad. *Maybe even more so.* The thought slipped in and Jennie pushed it away again.

"Me too, me too! Hannah squealed as she disengaged herself from Gram's lap and the porch swing and allowed Michael to scoop her into his arms.

While Jennie explained Mom's plan to stay at the hospital to Gram, she watched Michael roughhousing with the kids and Bernie on the grass.

"I'm sorry we have to put our plans on hold," Gram said. "Perhaps if your mother comes home early enough, I can take you out for tea at that new British Isles restaurant. I hear they serve wonderful scones with preserves and Devonshire cream."

"That would be great," Jennie heard herself saying. At the moment, food was the last thing on her mind. She dug into her bag, and after rummaging around for too long, came up with the keys to the Mustang. "I'd better get down to the police department before they decide to arrest me."

"Now don't you worry about that." Gram pulled her into a warm embrace. "You'll do fine."

Grandparents were wonderful people, Jennie decided as she maneuvered the car down the driveway and waved. You never had to prove yourself to them. They loved you just for breathing. And they believed in you. At least Gram did in her. While Mom wanted Jennie to go into anything but law enforcement, Gram took her seriously and had even coached her from time to time. She definitely needed to talk to Gram about Courtney.

By the time Jennie reached the police station the sky had turned a charcoal gray. She found a parking space two blocks away and raced to beat the downpour. Thunder cracked and lightning flashed as the sky opened up.

The drenched female reflected in the glass door bore little resemblance to the one she'd seen in the mirror earlier that morning, but he recognized her anyway.

"Hey, Jennie, you're wet." Dean Rockford, alias Rocky, chuckled and walked toward her.

"No kidding." Jennie tossed an easy grin his way. Rocky was her favorite cop. Frustrating as he could be at times, Jennie had gone from having a crush on him to thinking of him as a big brother and a good friend.

His laughing blue eyes turned serious. "I wondered if I'd run into you. Brown told me about seeing you last night. You're lucky it wasn't me. I'd have hauled you in."

"Yeah right." He might have too—if for nothing else than to protect her. He seemed to feel she needed looking after. "This isn't going to be another lecture is it?"

"Nah. As much fun as that sounds, I gotta get going. But I hope you take what happened to your friend seriously. How's she doing, by the way?"

Jennie told him.

He offered sympathies and said he'd see her later.

"Rocky?" she called as he reached the door. "Do you know who did it? I mean, do you have any suspects?"

"You never quit, do you Sherlock?"

"I just want to help. . . ." Now she *was* getting annoyed.

"Sorry, Jennie. You won't get a chance to play detective on this one. We're way ahead of you."

"What do you mean?"

"We're making an arrest this afternoon. Brown's probably collaring him right now."

"Him? Mr. Evans?"

Rocky took a step toward her. His blue eyes flashed with exasperation and admiration. "How do you do that?" He shook his head. "Never mind. Yeah. It's Evans. We got to checking for priors and hit pay dirt. Two years ago, Frank Evans was arrested, tried, and acquitted for his wife's murder."

13

Courtney lay under layers of white, looking more like snow than a rainbow.

A machine pumped air into her lungs through a tube secured to her mouth with a strip of tape. Two bags of liquid dripped into smaller tubes that wormed through a machine, joined at a Y, then disappeared under a bandage on Courtney's left wrist. White gauze covered her head, eliminating Courtney's colorful hair. They'd probably shaved it off, taking away her rainbow—her hope.

Jennie pressed a hand on the large plate glass window that separated them. A sign on the closed door read *No Visitors*.

The burden of guilt that Gram had lifted earlier in the day came back and settled on her like a coat of armor. Jennie felt a terrible sense of responsibility. *If you'd met Courtney at the mall after that first phone call, McGrady, maybe this wouldn't have happened.*

The guilt stretched beyond Courtney. Jennie shuddered, remembering the dazed look of disbelief on Frank Evans' face when the officers brought him into the police department. Jennie had just finished giving her statement. He'd seen her—or at least she thought he had. She'd expected him to be angry—he wasn't. Grief seemed to have etched deeper lines at the corners of his eyes and around his mouth. The gray in his sideburns seemed more prominent—as though he'd aged a dozen years since that morning.

Another lump made its way into Jennie's throat. Tears filled her eyes and dripped down her cheeks. "It isn't my fault," she whispered. "I didn't do anything wrong."

Curtains slid across the window, blocking Jennie's view of the room. She stepped back and felt someone's presence behind her. "Are you okay?" Michael's hands cupped her shoulders.

"No." She turned into his arms and buried her face in his shoulder. How could she be okay? She was crying her heart out over people she barely knew; and feeling like she had somehow brought it all about. Michael led her out of the ICU area, down the hall, and into another waiting room.

———

At four that afternoon, eyes dry and emotions under control, Jennie sat at a table near flouncey, white Victorian curtains. The window overlooked a quaint English garden in full bloom. She slathered rich whipped cream on a scone with raspberry jam and lifted it to her mouth. "Hmmm." She closed her eyes, savoring the taste and smells of the charming restaurant.

"It is good, isn't it?" Gram took several sips of her Earl Grey tea and settled her blue gaze on Jennie.

"Thanks for bringing me. I guess I needed to escape for a while. That business with Courtney and her dad was really getting to me."

"Such a tragedy."

"And Mom . . ." Jennie sighed. "I think she blames me for Frank's arrest."

"Oh no, Jennie. You mustn't think that. Susan is deeply hurt, but if she's upset with anyone, it's herself." Gram set her cup down and picked up her fork. "I imagine she's wondering how she could have been such a poor judge of character."

"Do you think she really loved Frank?"

Gram shook her head. "Only she can tell you that. I'm just thankful we found out about him now and not several months or years later."

"Yeah." Jennie frowned and broke off another piece of scone. Several crumbs dropped onto her new pink jeans. She brushed them off. "Do you think Frank did it?"

"Are you referring to his wife or Courtney?"

"Both, I guess."

"Well, he was acquitted of his wife's murder. It's up to a jury to decide whether or not he assaulted Courtney."

"Yeah, but what do you think?"

"From what I hear, the district attorney has a strong case against Frank. Did you know about the blood and hair samples the police found in the trunk of one of his cars?"

Jennie straightened. "No. Courtney's?"

"It looks that way, but they're still waiting for the final results from the lab."

"Who told you all that?" She took a sip of chamomile tea and returned the gold-trimmed floral teacup to its matching saucer.

Gram smiled. "I have my sources."

"Then I guess that means he's guilty."

Gram raised an eyebrow. "I gather you have some doubts."

"I don't know what to think. At first I really thought Frank had done it. Now that he's been arrested . . ." Jennie leaned back in the chair and tipped her head back.

"What is it, Jennie?" Gram leaned forward and rested her arms on the table. "What's troubling you?"

Jennie hesitated, trying to gather her stray thoughts into a semblance of order. "Something isn't right. I can feel it here." She balled up her hand and pressed it to her stomach.

Gram nodded. "Perhaps the police have been too hasty. Frank was acquitted of his wife's murder. Apparently there wasn't enough evidence to convict him. As to the evidence linking him to Courtney's assault, even if the blood and hair samples are hers, it only proves she was in the trunk, not that he put her there."

"And something else, Gram." Jennie's sagging heart stirred. "I just figured out what's been bothering me so much about this. Courtney called me about half an hour after Frank left the house. So how could he have had time to go downtown, find Courtney, and beat her up?"

Gram poured a fresh cup of tea from a calico cat teapot. Clear brown liquid streamed out of the cat's mouth. "Good point. But are you certain the caller was Courtney?"

"Yes . . . no. Not really. She didn't sound like herself. Her voice was raspy, like she had a cold or something. Or . . ." Jennie paused and rubbed her forehead. "Gram, you don't think it was someone impersonating her—wanting me to think she was safe—maybe someone who wanted to get me into the park to . . . to kill me?"

"Let's hope that's not the case. It's possible that someone wanted you to think Courtney was safe at that time—perhaps to establish an alibi."

"Mr. Evans? You mean like he could have had her hidden all the time?" Jennie blew out a long breath. "Wow. He could have staged the whole thing—made everyone believe Courtney was missing and then put on this grieving father act."

"I suppose that's possible, Jennie. But why would he want to bring attention to himself by copycatting the first murder?"

"What do you mean?"

Gram cleared her throat. "This isn't the best conversation to be having over tea," she said. "Perhaps we should wait until later."

Jennie set her empty plate aside. "I'm done. Tell me now."

Gram glanced around her and lowered her voice. "Frank

Evans' wife was beaten to death. Her body was found in a dumpster."

Gram was right about it not being a pleasant tea topic. Jennie took a deep breath to calm her queasy stomach.

"It just seems to me," Gram continued, her voice back to its normal volume, "that he wouldn't want to draw that kind of attention to himself."

"So you think someone's framing him? Maybe Frank has some enemies in the wrong places. Maybe some drug dealers were blackmailing him back in Boston and followed him out here."

"Hmmm." Gram brought the teacup to her lips, then lowered it. "That's an interesting scenario. I think I'll have another chat with my friends in the department. They may want to investigate the case more thoroughly. This sounds like the sort of thing the FBI and the DEA might want to know about."

Jennie had several other ideas but didn't voice them aloud. She wanted to talk to Tina again, and Gavin, Cassie, Joel, and Lisa, along with some of the other kids. If Frank hadn't assaulted Courtney, who had? And why?

"I see those wheels turning, Jennie. You're not thinking of doing anything foolish, are you? Your mother is very worried about you." Gram hesitated. "In fact, she asked if I'd have a chat with you about involving yourself in this case."

Jennie grimaced and heaved an exasperated sigh. "Not you too. Why does everyone feel it's their honor-bound duty to lecture me? I'm not stupid."

"That, my dear, is part of the problem. You are extremely intelligent. Being your grandmother I may be just a tad biased, but . . ." Gram smiled and lifted her hands and shoulders in a shrug.

Jennie rested her elbows on the table and her chin on her hands. "So what's the problem now? I said I was sorry about going out alone the other night. I know I should have let Mom know."

"I think that's as much my fault as it is yours." Gram hesitated as a waitress in a black shirtwaist dress and white ruffled apron set the check on the table.

"I do hope you enjoyed your time with us," she peeped in a distinct British accent. "Do come again."

"Thank you, Bridgette," Gram said as if she'd known the woman all her life instead of the hour they'd been there. "We will."

Gram tabled their conversation until after she had paid the bill and she and Jennie had gotten into the Mustang. "Now then," she said, buckling herself in. "Where were we?"

Jennie grinned at her. "You were telling me how brilliant I am. And you were about to lecture me for taking after you."

Gram brushed a hand through her salt-and-pepper hair. A look of sadness crossed her features. "You're right about that. I was a wild one. Losing my parents during the war didn't help. I must have driven my grandmother crazy with worry over whether or not I'd survive." Gram cleared her throat. "But enough of that. We were talking about you."

"Gram, please. I promise I won't do anything dangerous. I won't ever go downtown at night unless I have someone with me. And I'll tell Mom where I'm going. Okay?"

"One more thing." Gram placed her hand on Jennie's shoulder. "I know you want to investigate this matter with Courtney, and I'm not saying you can't ask questions. But if you find anything—promise you'll tell me, or your mother, or the police."

Jennie promised.

———

That night, after a quick dinner, Jennie scrambled into her car again, this time heading across town to Sunnyside.

"Hi, I wondered when you'd show up." Lisa tugged a

brush through her long wet tresses and frowned. "Gram told me you were coming. How's Courtney?"

"Not good. She's still in a coma. They don't know if she'll make it."

Lisa looked ten times better—still too thin, of course, but her skin had lost that gray look and the dark circles under her eyes were almost gone.

"Mom told me about Frank being arrested. That is just so awful." Lisa shuddered. A moment later, she set her brush down, scooted to the edge of the bed, and dangled her legs over the side.

"Did Courtney ever say anything to you about her dad hitting her?" Jennie asked.

Lisa shook her head. "I noticed a couple of bruises the last time I saw her. When I asked her about them, she brushed it off. Said she'd bumped her arm against a door."

"She told Cassie and Joel that her dad had hit her." Jennie retrieved a lone chair resting against the far wall, pulled it closer to Lisa's bed and dropped into it. "They think that's why she ran away."

"I don't blame her. I'd run away too."

"Yeah. If that's what happened."

"What do you mean? You think Courtney lied?"

Jennie shrugged. "I talked to Gram this afternoon and we . . . well, Mr. Evans might have been framed. I thought I'd ask a few questions. See if I can come up with some other suspects. Do you know if Courtney had any enemies? Anyone who'd want to beat her up?"

Lisa had grown strangely silent. Her eyes held a kind of wary look. She knew something.

"Lisa?"

"No." Her cousin scooted back into her bed and drew the covers over her. "I don't know anyone who would do something like that." She sighed. "I'm sorry, Jennie, but I'm afraid I'm not very good company yet. I'm really tired." She closed her eyes and turned her face to the wall away from Jennie. A lone tear trailed down her cousin's cheek and dripped onto the pale pink pajama top, creating a dime-sized splotch of rose.

Lisa was protecting someone. But who? And why?

14

"Why are you doing this?" Jennie asked, her voice unsteady and tinged with anger.

Lisa didn't respond.

"Talk to me, Lisa! Who are you trying to protect? Is it Brad? Joel?"

"No!" Lisa turned back to face Jennie. "Why can't you just leave it alone?"

"I can't. Courtney . . . if you could see her you'd understand. The police think her father did it and I thought so too at first, only now I'm not so sure. Please, tell me what you know."

Lisa stared at the white bedspread. "It's Courtney, okay? She's the one I wanted to protect—and me. I didn't want her to get into trouble. She . . . she gave me some diet pills. I promised I wouldn't tell."

"So she was dealing drugs."

"No. Not like that. I mean, not the bad stuff."

Not the bad stuff? Jennie struggled between blowing up at Lisa and not saying anything at all. She chose the latter, stuffed her hands in her jean pockets, spun around, and stalked out of the room.

Her stomach hurt. Her head hurt. She felt like she had lost her best friend. In a way she had. Sure, Lisa would always be her cousin, but she seemed to be drifting farther and farther away. First secretly starving herself, then this—this drug thing.

Jennie needed to talk to someone who was objective. And she needed to go back downtown to pay another visit to Tina. Even though she didn't consider six-thirty all that late, Jennie figured she'd better not go alone.

She stopped at a pay phone and called Gavin. He seemed anxious to talk to her as well and gave her directions to his house.

Twenty minutes later, Jennie pulled into a winding drive lined with trees. In less than a tenth of a mile the trees thinned, giving way to fenced pasture on both sides of the road. Two llamas peered at her for a moment, then went back to whatever they were eating. A big white barn sat near a two-story farmhouse atop a gently rolling hill. The white picket fence surrounding the house reminded Jennie of Tom Sawyer and Huck Finn.

Gavin stood in the driveway with a stream of water directed at a pair of black rubber boots that reached his knees. He waved as she drove in.

"Hi. I'll be with you in a minute. Had to milk Samantha and Erin." He nodded his head toward two goats penned up near the barn. "You can wait out here if you want, or come inside." He brushed the hair out of his eyes and grinned at her.

"I'll stay out here. I didn't know you lived on a farm."

"I wouldn't call it a farm exactly. It's more like my mom's hobby." Gavin wound the hose and dropped it on a hook beside the barn door. "I need to change. Be right back."

He jogged to the house, set his boots beside the front door, and disappeared inside. Jennie eyed the goats warily and walked toward them. They, being equally curious, approached the fence and bleated as though looking for a handout. "Sorry, kids, I don't have anything for you."

"Here." A woman appeared beside her and handed her

some carrots. "They love these."

Jennie took them. "Thanks. You must be Gavin's mom." The woman was about her own mother's age, maybe older. A leather clasp held most of her long dark brown hair in a tail at the back of her neck. The rest hung in wispy curls framing her face. With her ankle-length multicolored skirt and gauzy overblouse adorned with gold chains, she reminded Jennie of a gypsy.

"I'm Maddie, short for Madeline." She broke off the tops of the carrots she still held and waved them in front of the goats. "You're Jennie, right?"

Jennie nodded.

"From what I've read, you're a very brave young lady. I can see why Gavin admires you so much."

Jennie could feel her cheeks heat up. Not knowing what to say, she broke a carrot in half and handed a piece to each goat, then pulled her hand back when the animals nibbled at her fingers.

"I saw on the news that the police have arrested Frank Evans," Maddie went on. "Next thing you know he'll be getting out on bail. If you can afford to hire a lawyer you can get away with anything these days. The justice system makes no sense. I mean, what if he's guilty?"

Maddie looked at Jennie and laughed. "Oh, I'm sorry. I didn't mean to go on like that. It's a throwback to my political activist days. I see injustice and I go ballistic—at least that's what Gavin tells me. I used to carry protest signs and stage sit-ins during the Vietnam war. Then I married Steven. He's so straight he makes an arrow look warped. These days I write. Somehow it just isn't the same."

What if he is guilty? What if he does get out on bail? Mrs. Winslow's words seared Jennie's brain.

"Oh dear," Maddie said. "I'm boring you. I forget that kids today aren't all that interested in politics."

"What? Oh no, I'm sorry, I was just thinking about what

you said about Mr. Evans." Jennie shoved the information about Evans aside and tried to concentrate on what Gavin's mom was saying. "You're a writer?"

"Have been for quite some time. I write young adult novels. Mysteries."

"I love mysteries—read them all the time." Jennie frowned. "I don't remember seeing your name."

"I use a pseudonym. M.J. Curtis."

Jennie wished she could have said, *Oh wow, I've read all your books*, but couldn't. Truth is, she'd never heard of M.J. Curtis and had no idea what she'd written.

Maddie moved away from the fence, her warm smile still in place. "It's okay, Jennie. I'm not exactly on the bestseller list. Tell you what. I'll give you a copy of my newest release. You can read it and tell me what you think."

Maddie disappeared inside and an instant later Gavin appeared. He'd exchanged his denim overalls for a pair of black jeans and a white dress shirt, unbuttoned at the collar, shirtsleeves rolled up showing lean but muscular, suntanned arms. "Ready to go?"

"Yeah. Your mom's getting me a book."

Gavin rolled his eyes and gave her the old parents-can-be-so-embarrassing look.

Maddie emerged and glided toward them, presenting Jennie with an autographed copy of *Nice Day for a Murder*.

"Thanks."

"Um . . . Jennie, I'm not sure how to ask, so . . . well, I guess I just will. From all the things I've read about you, I think you'd make a wonderful character for a book and screenplay I'd like to do."

"Mo-om," Gavin groaned.

"No, really. I know you wanted to ask her yourself, but she's here and . . ." Maddie shrugged. "Anyway, Jennie. Think about it. Read my book, see if you like the style, and if you're interested, we'll do an interview."

Jennie was flattered. Who wouldn't be? "Why didn't you tell me?" Jennie asked Gavin as she backed the car around and headed down the drive.

"Didn't want to get your hopes up. Mom's not exactly famous, and to be honest I don't know if she can pull it off. I just didn't want you to go through all that for nothing."

"Hey, it's okay. Anyway, it doesn't really matter. What matters right now is finding out who might have beaten up Courtney. Have you seen her?"

Gavin nodded, his face grim. "I can't imagine anyone doing something like that." He glanced at Jennie and frowned. "Why are you still looking? The police arrested Evans."

Jennie explained her concerns about whether or not Frank was guilty.

"So you don't think he did it?"

"I don't know. It's all very confusing. Something tells me there's more to the case than what we're seeing. Which is why I want to talk to Tina again."

"Well, if Frank didn't do it, about the only thing that makes sense to me is that maybe a drug deal went sour or she got mixed up with some gang members." He slapped his knee. "This is crazy Jennie. I don't care what the police found on Courtney. She didn't do drugs."

"She might not have been taking drugs herself, but that doesn't mean she wasn't a supplier." Jennie considered telling him about Lisa and the diet pills but decided not to. "She had access to all kinds of things at the pharmacy." Jennie made a left on the main road and headed back toward the freeway.

"It's also possible," Jennie continued, "that someone was using Courtney to get to the drugs. Remember when we were looking for Courtney the night after she disappeared? Randy, the guy at the restaurant, and Tina both said Courtney was waiting for someone. I'd love to know who that person was."

"You think that might be the guy who assaulted Court-ney?"

"Who knows. I'd just like to come up with a list of likely suspects."

Gavin slid his hand back and forth across the shoulder strap of his seat belt. "You asked me if Courtney had any en-emies. I could only come up with one person who might hate her enough to want her dead. And that's Tracy Parouski."

"You can't be serious. Just because Courtney was chosen over her for rally squad? Gavin, you don't kill people for something like that."

"You wouldn't. It's not that important to you. But some kids would do anything to win."

Like Lisa, Jennie reminded herself. *Abusing her body so she could lose enough weight.*

Gavin shifted in his seat so that he faced Jennie more fully. "Remember that incident a few years ago in Texas where a girl's mother hired someone to kill a classmate so her daughter could become cheerleader?"

"Yes, but it was the girl's mother and she was crazy. . . ."

"Tracy really wants to be on the rally squad. Not only did she lose out to Courtney there, but—and this is where the plot thickens. . . ."

"Joel used to date Tracy," Jennie finished. "After you wrote the article on Courtney, Joel left Tracy in the dust. I see what you mean. I guess. Only from what I know of Joel, Tracy's the one who came out ahead on that one."

"What do you mean?"

Jennie told Gavin about Joel's making a pass at her that night on the bus. "He's some piece of work. Courtney's been missing for a few hours and he's already looking for someone else?"

"Maybe that's what makes him appealing."

Jennie grimaced. "Yeah, right."

They parked in a multi-level garage above the *Real Mother*

Goose Art Gallery downtown and headed east, past Nordstrom and into Pioneer Square. An hour and what felt like ten miles later, they headed into The Eatery to wait. Randy, still trying to keep his narrow swatch of pale yellow hair out of his eyes, took their orders and their money.

"If you're still looking for Tina, I wouldn't hold my breath. Folks around here are not too likely to talk to you. Not after what happened to Courtney."

"We had nothing to do with that," Jennie said. "In fact, that's why we're here. We're trying to find out who Courtney was meeting that night."

He set two large glasses of kiwi-strawberry juice and a thick crust pepperoni pizza on the counter. "I can tell you that."

Jennie's head jerked up. "You can?"

"Yeah. Maybe." Randy tipped his head forward and back, flinging his tail temporarily out of the way. "After Tina and Courtney left that night, a big guy came in—about six foot, two hundred and fifty pounds. He looked around and left."

A picture of Joel flashed through her mind. "Why didn't you tell us before?"

"I didn't make the connection before."

"And you didn't tell the police?"

"You kidding?" He wiped the counter with a rag and tossed it into a basin. "I don't talk to the cops unless I have to. Besides, they arrested her old man so I figure it doesn't matter."

"This guy," Gavin said, "do you remember anything else about him, other than he was big? Hair color, eyes?"

Randy scrunched up his face, then shook his head. "Like I said, he just came in and out. I wouldn't have even connected him with her except, you know, when something bad happens you start to remember things."

"Do you remember anything else?"

"I'll let you know."

They thanked him for the information and found an empty table near the entrance so they'd be able to see Tina if she came in or walked by.

"You thinking what I'm thinking?" Gavin peeled the paper from his straw and dropped it into his drink.

"That it might have been Joel?"

Gavin nodded. "Only that doesn't make a lot of sense. If he wanted to talk to Courtney, why didn't he do it when he took her home? They'd gone out that night."

"Yeah, unless he was helping her run away. Maybe he dropped her off and came back."

"Or maybe it was someone else." Gavin pulled in half the drink in two gulps. "In case you hadn't noticed, there are a lot of guys built like trees in this town. Could be someone from the college."

"It could be anyone."

The restaurant door swung open and Tina backed in. Gavin jumped up to hold it for her.

"I got it," she said. "Thanks anyway."

She was still wearing the leather jacket, but instead of the yellow tank top and jeans, she wore a red denim miniskirt and red shirt that tied in the front. She turned to face Jennie and crutch-walked toward her. "I hear you wanted to see me."

Jennie smiled and pulled out the chair beside her. "I am so glad you decided to come. We're trying to piece together what happened to Courtney."

"First, you gotta know—she wasn't on no drugs. I don't care what the cops found."

"I agree," Gavin said. "If Courtney had drugs, somebody planted them on her."

"You got that right." A tray appeared in front of Tina and she tore away at the wrapping and bit into the burger.

"When we talked before, you said Courtney took care of you. What did you mean?" Jennie asked.

Tina stopped chewing and swallowed. Her ebony gaze

shifted from Jennie to Gavin and back again. "I guess it won't hurt to tell you now, but it probably don't have nothin' to do with what happened to her."

Tina set her hamburger down and took a deep breath. "I got diabetes. Courtney says that's why I got this sore on my foot. She kep' saying, 'Tina, you got to see a doctor.' Humph—ain't no way I'd do that—they ask too many questions. Anyway, she started bringing me stuff—bandages, antibiotics—stuff to keep me from gettin' gan'grene. She brought me syringes and insulin. Now I don't know what I'm gonna do."

Not the bad stuff. Lisa had said. "How many other kids had Courtney helped?" Jennie wondered aloud.

Tina shrugged, picking a piece of lettuce out of a salad Randy had given her. "She never told me, an' I never asked."

"What about the guy she was supposed to meet?" Gavin adjusted his glasses. "Randy said he thought it might have been the guy he saw come in the night before we talked to you. Big guy."

Tina nodded. "Yeah. I know who he means. When you guys came in that night after Courtney disappeared, you wanted to know who he was. I didn't want to tell you. He and his friends was handin' out the same flyer on Courtney as you. I thought maybe you were workin' together. Courtney was scared of him. She told me she couldn't give him what he wanted."

Joel. The name burned in Jennie's mind. "Did he have dark hair and brown eyes?"

Tina frowned and shook her head. "Nope. This guy had light hair. Name started with a 'B'."

Jennie sucked in her breath. No, it couldn't be. Not . . . She must have said his name out loud because Tina plunked her glass on the table.

"Brad. Yeah. That's it, girl. His name was Brad."

15

"Are you sure?" A slow burn started in the pit of Jennie's stomach and spread outward. She stared at her hands in disbelief. Why? Why would Brad meet Courtney after her date with Joel? Why would he meet her at all?

"Do you have a picture of him?" Tina asked. "I'd know him if I saw him."

Jennie rummaged through her bag. She did have some snapshots in her wallet but couldn't remember if Brad was in any of them. Jennie flipped through the plastic-cased photos. Lisa and her in a photo booth. Kurt and Nick sticking out their tongues at the camera. Mom and Michael. Dad. There. Lisa and Brad in another photo booth. She freed the picture from its plastic protector and handed it to Tina.

It took the girl all of two seconds to make a positive ID.

A few minutes later, Jennie murmured a thank you to Tina as she and Gavin left the restaurant.

"Whew," Gavin whistled once they were out on the sidewalk. "I never expected that. Do you think Brad and Courtney were seeing each other on the side?"

"All I know is that Brad Lewis has a lot of explaining to do."

Jennie dropped Gavin back at his house then headed home. The clock on the dash read 9:05. When she reached the freeway, Jennie considered driving over to the hospital to see her cousin.

111

She needed to talk to Lisa about Brad.

Maybe you'd better not, McGrady, she mused. *Lisa's pretty fragile right now. If Brad had been secretly seeing Courtney, the news would break her heart and maybe set her back.*

The best course of action, Jennie decided, was to talk to Brad before saying anything to Lisa. After all, Brad may have had a perfectly good reason for meeting Courtney.

Nick, Hannah, and Bernie attacked her the moment she walked in the door. Mom asked her to bathe the kids and get them ready for bed so she could get some work done for a client. Almost glad for the distraction, Jennie set her talk with Brad on hold.

"So," Jennie grinned at her two charges. "You two need a bath, huh? Should I take you out in the backyard and hose you down?"

"Jennie," Mom warned. "Don't get them all riled up. They're supposed to be settling down for the night."

"Slave driver," Jennie teased. "Well, you guys heard her. Who's first?"

"Me! Me!" they yelled in unison. Jennie picked them both up around the waist and carried them like sacks of flour up the stairs and into the bathroom. An hour later, she quietly closed the bedroom door and went in search of Mom. Jennie found her in the study, still working on the computer.

"You planning on making this an all-nighter?" Jennie asked, planting a light kiss on Mom's cheek.

Mom glanced at her watch. "No, another hour or so should do it. Thanks for your help, sweetie."

"No problem." Jennie started to leave, then swung around. "Mom?"

"Hmmm."

"We haven't gotten a chance to talk about Frank's arrest. You were there when the police picked him up at the hospital, weren't you?"

"Yes." Mom closed her eyes for a moment. "But if you

don't mind, I'd rather not talk about it right now."

"I just wondered how you felt about it, that's all."

"Jennie," Mom peered at her as if trying to decide whether or not to answer. "It doesn't change anything. Frank had already told me about his wife's murder and the trial. The jury found him innocent."

Not exactly innocent. They acquitted him for insufficient evidence. There's a difference. Jennie thought about arguing the point, but decided against it.

"I guess I can understand why the police might suspect him, though," Mom went on.

"But you think he's innocent?"

"Innocent?" Mom bit her bottom lip as though weighing her words, then finally said, "Yes, I do."

Jennie nodded. "Hmmm."

"I hope you don't plan on trying to change my mind." Mom brushed her bangs aside. Her eyes looked tired.

"No. At least not right now. I just wondered." Jennie considered asking her if she still planned to date Frank, then decided not to. "I'll be in my bedroom."

Mom said good-night, blew Jennie a kiss, and turned back to the computer screen.

Once in her room, Jennie took a pad and pen from her desk drawer and tucked her long slender form into a window seat. After fluffing several cushions behind her she leaned back and let her mind drift over the people and events of the last few days.

A few minutes later, with the long side of the paper at the top, she wrote "Suspects in the Courtney Evans Case." She then drew a horizontal line and four vertical lines. Between each line she wrote Suspects/Enemies, Relationship, Motive, Means, and Opportunity.

Frank Evans' name topped the list. Even after her talk with Gram, Jennie still considered him a suspect. The evidence against him was too strong to discount. Under relationship, she wrote, "Father." Motive? "Caught Courtney stealing drugs from the pharmacy."

Means? "Fists, maybe a blunt instrument of some sort." Jennie shuddered at the thought of it. *Come on, McGrady. You're losing your objectivity.* Jennie took a deep breath and went on.

Opportunity? That was the hard one. Frank had left their house only half an hour before Courtney's call asking Jennie to meet her. He had opportunity only if he knew exactly where to find her. *Or,* Jennie reminded herself, *if he'd had her hidden and forced Courtney to make the call.* But why?

Remembering her conversation with Gram, she wrote, "To establish an alibi."

Jennie drew a line under the entry she'd just made, then wrote, "Tracy." Definitely an enemy. Motive? *Jealousy—on two counts—Joel and cheerleading.* Means? *Tracy couldn't have beaten Courtney like that—at least not alone.* Jennie tapped her pen against the paper. *But she could have hired someone.* Beside Tracy's name she wrote "Hit man" and followed it with a large question mark.

She listed Brad next. Jennie wondered again about his relationship to Courtney. Before talking to Tina she'd have guessed they were just friends.

Jennie had a hard time picturing him as a cold-blooded killer. And that's what they were dealing with. Courtney may have come out of that dumpster alive, but someone obviously wanted her dead.

Unable to answer the questions on Brad, Jennie decided to fill them in after she talked to him and Lisa.

She thought about listing Tina. Courtney's diabetic friend couldn't have done it and certainly didn't seem to have a motive. *But...*what if Tina's gang member friends had? What if Courtney had been supplying them with drugs, then cut them off? A definite possibility. Under names, Jennie wrote "Drug Users/ Dealers." She had no problem defining motive, means, and opportunity. They had plenty.

Jennie was about to set her chart aside for the night when another possibility came to her. Gavin Winslow. She frowned and shook her head, discounting it at first. *Think about it, McGrady*, she told herself. *He says he's Courtney's friend. She dumps him for Joel. He's hurt and angry.* "He's not all that strong," Jennie argued against her own logic. Could he have beat Courtney up and tossed her body into a dumpster? *Maybe.*

The phone rang before Jennie could pursue the thought any further.

"It's me, Lisa," a soft voice whispered. "I need to talk to you. Can you come over?"

"Now?"

"Tomorrow, as soon as you can get here."

"Can't you tell me over the phone?" Jennie asked.

Silence.

"Lisa? Are you still there?"

"I . . . I'm sorry I got so upset with you this morning. I was wrong to take those diet pills. I've been wrong about a lot of things lately."

She waited for Lisa to go on. When she didn't, Jennie asked, "Do you want me to come now?"

"Yes, but you can't. Mom would have a fit. She's upset because I went for a drive with Brad after dinner. I'm not even supposed to be calling you."

"Your mom? Brad? You're at home?"

"Didn't your mom tell you?"

"Apparently not." Jennie considered being upset with Mom then cancelled the thought. Some things just weren't worth fighting over. "So what's going on?"

"The doctor discharged me this afternoon. Said I could go if I promised to behave myself. I will. Believe me, I have no intention of landing back in the hospital."

Jennie wanted to ask her about Brad, but didn't. Lisa

needed her rest. Tomorrow would be soon enough.

————

The next morning Jennie packed up Nick, Hannah, and Bernie and headed for Lisa's. She hadn't wanted to bring them, but it was either that or baby-sit at the house while Mom worked.

When Jennie drove up, Kate was turning off the sprinklers in the front yard. "Hi," she called as they piled out of the car. Kate met them halfway up the walk and gave each a hug, then bent down to pet Bernie.

"Where's Kurt?" Nick asked.

"In the backyard, I think."

"C'mon Hannah. Let's go play." Nick grabbed Hannah's hand and ran through the wet grass and disappeared around the corner of the house.

Kate put an arm around Jennie's shoulder. "I have some good news for you—at least I think it will be. Kurt's been begging me to take him swimming all week so Gram and I thought this would be a good day for it."

Jennie couldn't help but smile at her aunt's enthusiasm. Sometimes Kate went on like a wind-up toy with a battery that keeps going . . . and going.

"We'll take the kids out to Blue Lake for a picnic," Kate went on. "You and Lisa can come if you want, but I think Lisa would just as soon spend some time with you alone. She's upstairs if you want to talk to her about it."

"Thanks." Jennie gave her aunt another hug. "Um, Aunt Kate? Is Lisa going to be okay?"

Concern shaded Kate's dark blue eyes. "I hope so. She seemed in good spirits yesterday afternoon, but after being with Brad last night she looked . . . I don't know. Kind of sullen." Kate frowned. "Maybe she was just tired. Anyway, she's excited about spending the day with you." Kate squeezed Jennie's shoulder. "You watch out for her, okay?

Make sure she doesn't overdo it."

"Sure—at least I'll try." Jennie glanced toward the house. "Where's Gram? I want to talk to her before you go."

"You just missed her. She went to run a few errands and pick up some groceries for our picnic. Said she'd meet me out at the park around noon. If it's really important I can have her call you from the lake."

"No, that's okay. I'll talk to her later." Jennie was disappointed. She'd hoped to tell Gram about her chart of suspects. Jennie also wanted Gram's input before broaching the subject of Brad and Courtney with Lisa.

"Talk to who?" Lisa asked as she came down the front steps to join them. Her cheeks had filled out and although she was still too thin, she'd lost that haunting, hungry look.

"Gram," Jennie answered, then changed the subject. "So what do you want to do today?"

Lisa, as Kate predicted, didn't want to go to the lake. "I'd like to stay here for a while. And maybe this afternoon we could go to the school and watch football practice." Lisa gave Jennie a please-go-along-with-me look.

"Staying here is fine, Lisa," Kate said. "Only I'm not sure I want you going over to the school. Your short date with Brad last night wore you out."

Lisa flinched. "I wasn't tired. We . . ." Lisa hesitated and sighed. "We had a minor disagreement, that's all. I feel great this morning and I promise . . . swear on a stack of Bibles, that I won't overdo it."

Kate wrapped her arms around Lisa. "It's not that I don't want you to have fun, honey. I just want you safe and healthy."

Lisa returned the hug. "I know, Mom. I want to get well too."

"All right." Kate drew back. "But remember what the doctor said. And don't forget to eat."

The moment everyone left, Lisa dragged Jennie through

the house and into the kitchen. After fixing two glasses of lemonade, they continued out to the backyard to an enormous wooden deck. Though the house was located in a residential area, their two-acre lot gave the appearance of a country setting. The landscaping Aunt Kate and Uncle Kevin had done afforded lots of privacy.

Lisa and Jennie settled onto padded redwood chairs under arbors of grape and wisteria and surrounded by containers overflowing with impatiens, begonias, lobelia, and just about every other flower known to humankind. It seemed like the kind of place to be discussing love and peace and happiness. Certainly not the near murder of a classmate.

Jennie sipped at her juice wondering how to start. A lot of questions came to mind, like, *How well do you know Brad Lewis? Did you know he met Courtney downtown the night she supposedly ran away? No, McGrady. You need to be more subtle.*

"Something's wrong with Brad," Lisa said.

Then again, maybe not. Jennie set her glass on the redwood table beside her. "What do you mean?"

"I noticed it after he got back from football camp. I'm worried, Jennie. He's acting different. I tried to talk to him about it last night and he got mad at me. I mean really mad."

"Lisa . . ." Jennie hesitated, not certain as to how to proceed. "Um . . . did he hit you?"

Lisa bit her lip and stared at her glass as tears filled her sea green eyes.

16

"He didn't mean to. He apologized right after." Lisa went into the house and came back a few seconds later, clutching a tissue in her hand.

Jennie swallowed hard to stem the rising anger. "You shouldn't be making excuses for him. Has he ever hit you before?"

"No, of course not. I'd have told you."

"What happened?"

"We'd gone for a drive and he wanted to go up to Council Crest to watch the lights and . . . you know."

Jennie nodded. "Let me guess. He wanted more than kisses and you said no. He got mad."

Lisa took a deep, shuddering breath. "I was scared, Jen. He's never acted like that before. I got out of the car and he came after me. He yelled at me and kept pushing me back. I fell down and started crying. I guess that shook him up, because he stopped and apologized. After that he was really nice."

"Did you break up with him?"

"No." Lisa frowned. "Not yet. I like him a lot—at least I did." Lisa tipped her head back against the chair and closed her eyes. "Oh, Jen, I don't know what to do."

"Do you think he might be doing drugs?" Jennie asked, remembering the meeting he'd had with Courtney.

Lisa looked up, startled. "No . . . I mean, he'd never do that. The coach would kick him off the team in a second. Besides, he's a total health nut. Why would you even ask? I mean . . . I know a lot of kids use—even some of the athletes, but not Brad."

Here's your chance, McGrady. Jennie inhaled a deep breath and blew it out her mouth, then told Lisa the entire story.

When Jennie finished, Lisa loosened her grip on the chair. "You think Brad beat her up?"

"I think we need to talk to him."

Lisa nodded and stared straight ahead. "I can see why you asked about the drugs. I guess it's either that or he was seeing her on the side. I'm not sure which hurts worse."

"I was going to call him this morning," Jennie said, "and arrange a meeting. You want to be there when I talk to him?"

"Definitely." Lisa glanced at her watch. "He's working right now. But he should be home for lunch in about twenty minutes, then he'll be at football practice for the rest of the afternoon. If we head over to his house now, maybe we can catch him before he leaves again."

Jennie and Lisa had been waiting at the curb in front of Brad's house for only a few minutes when a battered white pickup with a *Lewis Landscaping* logo pulled into the driveway. The girls got out of the car and started toward it.

Brad jumped out of the truck and smiled when he saw them. "Hi." His smile melted into a question. "What are you guys doing here? I mean, it's not that I'm not glad to see you or anything, but this isn't a very good time. I have to shower and eat and get to practice."

He pulled off a soiled sleeveless denim shirt and used it to wipe perspiration from his forehead. It left a streak of dirt an inch wide on his angular cheek.

"We'd like to ask you a few questions about Courtney,"

Lisa began. "It shouldn't take very long."

He tossed the shirt into the back of the truck. "Look, I don't know anything about Courtney or about what happened to her. And I don't have time to play detective. I'll talk to you later, okay?"

He started to walk away and Lisa stepped in front of him, her green eyes flashing. "No, it's really not okay. One of the homeless kids Jennie talked to said you met Courtney downtown the night she supposedly ran away. That was the same night you came to see me at the hospital with Courtney and Joel. What I want to know is why you were meeting her so late. If you had things to say to each other, why didn't you say them earlier?"

Brad shook his head and pushed past Lisa. "I don't know what you're talking about. Whoever told you that was wrong. I haven't seen Courtney since she and Joel dropped me off Wednesday night. As far as I know she ran away." He turned to Jennie. "You heard what Cassie said about Courtney's old man."

"Don't lie to me, Brad." Lisa balled her hands into fists and folded her arms.

Brad turned around. "I told you—"

"I haven't said anything to the police yet," Jennie interrupted. "I wanted to hear your side of the story first."

Brad hesitated, then came back toward them. Hostility glinted in his steel blue eyes. "Okay, I did talk to Courtney that night, but I didn't have anything to do with her getting beat up."

"Why did you meet her?" Jennie asked.

"She called me. She wanted to talk to me about Joel." Brad turned to Lisa. "You have to believe that, Lis. Courtney was goin' with Joel. Besides, she's not my type. And I didn't do anything to hurt her."

"You hit Lisa last night," Jennie said. "Why should we believe you didn't beat up Courtney?"

"You told her?" Brad glowered at Lisa. He clenched his fist and took a step toward her.

Lisa straightened to her full five feet, two inches. "Go ahead. Hit me. Make my day."

Jennie winced. Her cousin was definitely improving. "I'd think twice about doing anything like that, Brad. Unless you'd like to spend the afternoon at the police station."

Brad glanced nervously from Lisa to Jennie and lowered his arm. "I wasn't going to hit anybody."

"What did you and Courtney talk about?" Lisa asked.

"I told you. She wanted to talk to me about Joel."

"What about him?" Jennie pressed.

"Okay, I promised I wouldn't tell anyone, but . . . I guess after all that's happened it doesn't really matter. She and Joel hadn't been getting along too good and she wanted some advice. I told her that things had been kind of tough for all us guys lately. Coach Haskell's been coming down on us real hard." Brad shifted from one foot to the other. "Anyway, Lis, you don't have to worry. We're still goin' together—aren't we?"

Lisa took a deep breath and shook her head. "I don't know, Brad. I honestly don't know."

"Look, I swear, I didn't have anything to do with what happened to Courtney. I didn't beat her up. You . . . you're not going to tell the police about that meeting, are you?"

"If you're innocent, you don't have anything to worry about," Jennie answered.

As Jennie turned to head back to the car, Brad grabbed her arm and spun her around. "There's more to it than that. If Coach Haskell finds out, he'll kick me off the team."

"What do you want us to do, Brad, forget it?" Jennie pulled her arm out of his grasp.

"All I'm saying is that the police have already arrested Frank Evans. Telling them about my meeting with Courtney wouldn't make any difference to their case, and it could ruin me."

"I'll think about it," Jennie said, backing away from him. "In the meantime, you'd better hustle or you'll be late for practice."

"Are you going to tell the police about Brad?" Lisa asked as they pulled away from the curb.

"Yeah, but first I want to talk to Joel. According to Brad, Joel and Courtney weren't getting along. Do you think he's telling the truth?"

"I wish I could say yes, but I don't know. Courtney did seem preoccupied that night, but I didn't get the impression that she was mad at Joel or anything." Lisa leaned her head against the seat and frowned. "Do you think maybe Joel beat her up?"

Jennie shrugged.

"We've known Joel and Brad for a long time, Jen. They're Christians. I just can't imagine either of them hurting Courtney like that."

"I know. But somebody sure did, and I'd really like to find out who."

"Why are you so sure it isn't her dad?"

"I'm not. I just can't get over the feeling that something else is going on. Gram thinks so too. It may be nothing, but I feel like I have to keep digging."

Jennie and Lisa stopped for hamburgers before going to football practice. Lisa protested, but Jennie insisted she eat. By the time they got to the school, Coach Haskell had half the team charging dummies and the other half trying to dance through a bunch of old tires—to condition themselves and improve their footwork, she'd been told.

Several kids were sitting in the bleachers as Jennie and Lisa approached. Tracy and her best friend, Corky, sat at the top and ignored Lisa's greeting. "She makes me so mad," Lisa muttered. "DeeDee gave Tracy Courtney's spot on the rally squad and Allison says she's been a total snob ever since."

Jennie leaned toward her cousin and whispered, "I've got her on my suspect list."

"Really?" Lisa seemed pleased by the prospect.

"Gavin suggested it. Said she'd do anything to get on the rally squad. By hiring some thug to get rid of Courtney, a spot opens up and she gets revenge at the same time."

"I take it you plan on questioning her too."

"You got it."

Cassie Nielsen, who was sitting near Gavin, greeted them as they approached. Faded denim cutoffs and a white T-shirt and cap showed off a healthy-looking tan. "Brad told us you'd gotten out of the hospital, Lisa. How are you doing?"

"Good," Lisa said. "I'm getting stronger all the time."

"Super." Cassie smiled, then turned serious. Her brown eyes widened in concern. "Listen, when the doctor says you're ready, you'll have to come over to the house. My dad will help us get you on a fantastic fitness program. He has this computer software that creates a plan exactly right for your age and body type. You don't have to diet to be in great shape. It's all got to do with attitude. Like Dad says, 'Treat your body like a temple and it'll be a great place to live.'"

Lisa sat down next to Cassie, and Jennie went up a couple of rows to where Gavin was fiddling with the lens on his camera.

"I thought you might show up here." He lowered the camera and looked at her with a smile.

"Lisa and I stopped to talk to Brad," Jennie explained as she sat on the bleacher in front of him.

His eyebrows shot up. "Yeah? What did old Brad have to say for himself?"

Jennie repeated their conversation. "So," she said when she'd finished, "I guess the next step is to find out if Joel and Courtney were having some problems."

Cassie twisted around and lifted a tan muscular leg over to straddle the bench. "Why do you want to know about Joel and Courtney?"

Jennie told her about Tina seeing Brad with Courtney and reiterated their conversation with Brad.

"I don't know why Brad would say something like that." Cassie sighed. "I mean . . . Joel and Courtney were getting along great. Not like they were thinking of getting married or anything, but they're friends—good friends."

She sighed again and ran a hand through her short brown hair. "Wow. Brad was seeing Courtney? That surprises me." She switched her gaze from Jennie to Lisa. "You must be totally bummed out."

"I'm numb." Lisa straightened and tucked strands of auburn ringlets behind her ear.

"Yeah. I can understand that." Cassie shook her head, apparently still having trouble assimilating the information. She looked up suddenly, light dawning in her chocolate eyes. "Wait a minute." She pointed a finger at Jennie. "You think Brad or Joel had something to do with Courtney's getting beat up, don't you?"

"The thought had occurred to me."

"Well, you can forget that," Cassie erupted. "I know these guys. If they were into anything even remotely out of line, I'd know about it."

Cassie's anger fizzled. "There's something you should know before you go around making accusations. Joel and Brad wouldn't do anything to jeopardize the team. They live, breathe, eat, and sleep sports. In fact, now that I think about it, maybe Courtney did want to talk to Brad about Joel. Maybe she was upset about the amount of time Joel spends working out and stuff."

"You really think so?" Lisa asked.

"Yeah, I bet that's it," Cassie agreed. "Besides, Lisa, Brad's always talking about you. When you were in the hospital he about went crazy with worry." Obviously pleased with her conclusion, she continued, "Whatever happened to Courtney couldn't have had anything to do with Brad or Joel."

Jennie wound her long ponytail around her hand. "Cassie? I was just wondering. You seemed to know Courtney pretty well. Was she into drugs?"

Cassie glanced around, then whispered, "I'm not a narc, but since the police already found stuff on her, I guess I can tell you. When Joel first started dating her, I'm sure she was clean. Then she started having more and more trouble with her dad. I can't say for sure . . . I mean, she never took anything around me or Joel but I wasn't surprised when the cops found it. With her dad owning the pharmacy and everything, it would be pretty easy for her to get whatever she wanted."

Jennie agreed.

On the field, the guys finished their workouts and were starting their scrimmage. They'd separated into two groups.

"They're looking good," Gavin said. "Even bigger and stronger than last year."

Jennie winced as number 47 tackled number 23 and about a dozen others piled on top. Talk about overkill. Cassie had made another good observation, Jennie decided. Joel and Brad loved sports.

Jennie glanced back at Tracy. The girls were giggling and didn't seem particularly interested in what was happening on the field. A good time to ask a few questions. "Be back in a minute," Jennie said to whoever might have been listening.

By the time she'd come within twenty feet of them, Tracy and Corky had stopped talking. They watched her approach and Jennie tried to ignore their frosty glares.

"What do you want, McGrady?" Tracy asked.

"Bet she's trying to play detective again," Corky said.

"Not a bad guess, Corky—except for the playing part. Believe me, this is no game."

Tracy rolled her eyes in disgust. "Get real, Jennie. The cops have already solved the case, so why don't you go home?"

Keep your cool, McGrady, Jennie told herself. *Don't let them get to you.* "I'm surprised at your attitude, Tracy. Remember what the Bible says about loving your neighbor? I don't see a lot of love coming from you two." Jennie usually didn't resort to preaching. Probably because she hated being preached at. But if anyone needed a sermon on love, these two did.

Jennie stood next to Tracy. She thought about sitting down, but decided not to. She struck a much more commanding pose by standing. In an attempt to look relaxed, Jennie set one foot a rung higher than the other and rested her arm on her bent leg. "What if I told you the police have the wrong person and with more evidence coming in, they're looking at other possibilities?"

"Oh yeah," Tracy sneered. "And like you'd know."

"What I know, Tracy Parouski, is that you are a prime suspect." Jennie didn't bother telling Tracy that she had drawn up the suspect list, not the police.

Tracy stiffened. *Good going, McGrady. You have her attention.* "I happen to know," Jennie continued, "that you had a pretty strong motive for wanting Courtney out of the way."

"That—that's crazy."

"Is it?" Jennie raised her eyebrows. *So far so good.* "My sources tell me you hated Courtney for taking Joel away from you. To make matters even worse, she was chosen over you for rally squad. Sounds like motive to me." Jennie moved what she hoped was a steady gaze from Tracy to Corky. "Don't you think so, Corky?"

Corky stared at Tracy, her mouth open. "You didn't . . ."

Tracy made an indignant huffing sound. "Of course not."

"Give me one good reason why I should believe you. You're the only one around here who would benefit with

Courtney out of the picture. And you certainly don't seem to be shedding any tears."

"I feel bad about what happened to Courtney," Tracy admitted. "But hey, she was doing drugs—she got what she deserved. I'm not going to pretend I feel bad about replacing her on rally. I don't. In fact, I'm thrilled. And as far as Joel's concerned, she can have him."

Now it was Jennie's turn to be surprised. "Really? I was under the impression you liked him."

"I did, at first. Who wouldn't? He's cute and built like a rock." Tracy looked out on the field. "But he's mean. When things don't go his way, he . . ."

An idea began to form in Jennie's mind. Why hadn't she thought of it before? Jennie watched the players with renewed interest. What was it Gavin had said? *They're bigger and stronger than ever.* Brad and Joel were the biggest guys on the team. In less than a year, they'd gone from being mediocre players to being pro material. They were dedicated to sports all right. Maybe too dedicated.

Excitement pumped through Jennie's veins like a raging river. She was finally on to something.

17

"Steroids," she murmured under her breath. *Joel and Brad were using steroids.*

"What did you say?" Tracy asked, looking from Jennie to the field of players.

"Nothing." She straightened and turned to go. "Thanks, Tracy. You've been a great help."

Jennie hurried back to where Gavin, Cassie, and Lisa were sitting, anxious to break the news. *Wait a minute, McGrady,* she stopped. *You can't say anything—not yet. You have no proof. An accusation like that could ruin the team and it might not be true. Besides, hadn't Cassie insisted that if the guys were into drugs she'd know?* Maybe she did know.

No. Wait. You're jumping to conclusions. Jennie needed to get away—to think things through. Steroids. That could explain Brad's clandestine meeting with Courtney. Was she supplying them? Had she cut them off? Had her dad found out about it?

The questions filled her mind faster than she could process them. Jennie needed to talk to Frank Evans and . . . the note Courtney had written and slipped to Jennie. It had the name of a drug on it. *Dianabol.* Had that been a clue?

"Well," Gavin asked when she approached. "Did she do it?"

"What?"

"Tracy. You just talked to her. What did you find out?"

Jennie shrugged her shoulders. "Not much. I hate to break this up, guys, but I've got to go. Lisa? Are you ready?"

Jennie had expected an argument, but Lisa said, "Sure," and followed Jennie down the bleachers.

"Are you okay?" Jennie asked, waiting at the bottom of the risers for Lisa to catch up.

"Yeah, I'm kind of tired."

"Maybe we shouldn't have come out here. You're not going to pass out on me again, are you?"

"No, really. I'm fine. I just need to rest for a while."

———————

Jennie dropped Lisa off at her house at a few minutes before two, fixed her a snack, then headed for the library. She had desperately wanted to talk to Lisa about her suspicions, but was afraid Lisa would want to go with her. Jennie had no intention of being responsible for another relapse.

Once inside, she headed for a pay phone and called her mother to report in. Mom seemed pleased with Jennie's location. She might have had another reaction had she known what Jennie had gone there for.

"Mom," Jennie said, suddenly remembering another piece of the bizarre puzzle. "When you first started doing Frank's books he said something about a discrepancy in them. Did you ever find out what that was?"

Mom hesitated. "I'm not sure. After the police found drugs on Courtney, Frank was afraid she might have taken some of the narcotics and sold them. We checked the inventory against the billings from the pharmaceutical companies and those drugs were all accounted for. Why are you asking?"

"You might want to try some of the other stuff—like insulin, diet pills, and—steroids."

"Now, how would you know . . . Jennie, you're not . . ."

"Relax, Mom. I'm not in any trouble—or danger. I was

just talking to some of the kids. One of the street kids said Courtney had been giving her insulin. I'm just guessing on the others."

Mom sighed. "You're sure you're at the library?"

That annoyed her. "Yes," she said a little more harshly than necessary. "Do you want me to have the librarian call you to verify it?"

"I'm sorry, Jennie. I believe you. It's just . . . well, after what happened to Courtney."

"I'm fine, mom. Don't be such a worry wart. You know what Jesus said about not being anxious." Jennie winced at her own words. Quoting scripture twice in one day. You'd think she was headed for seminary instead of law school.

"He didn't have a daughter like you."

"I'm sorry I'm such a disappointment. I gotta go. Bye." Jennie hung up before her mom could say anything more.

For the next hour Jennie used computers to hunt down articles, books, and drug resources that might help her strengthen her theory.

"Hi." A familiar leather bag appeared next to a pile of books she'd pulled from the shelves.

Jennie almost jumped off her chair. "Gavin. What are you doing here? Did you follow me?"

"On my bike? You kidding?" He slid onto the chair next to hers. "I called your house. Your mom told me where you were. She's not disappointed."

"What?"

"Your Mom . . . she said, 'Tell Jennie I'm not disappointed.' Said you'd know what she meant."

"Oh." The corners of her mouth lifted in a smile. "I knew that."

"Whatever." He gave her a look that questioned her sanity, then nodded at her research project. "In case you hadn't noticed, school doesn't start until September."

"This isn't about school." She frowned. "It's about Courtney."

"Why am I not surprised? I knew you had something cooking when you left the school in such a hurry. Frankly, I'm hurt you didn't tell me. What is it?" His gaze roamed over the papers and books scattered over the table's surface.

"Just a hunch."

Gavin let out a low whistle. "Steroids? Jennie, I'm impressed. I can see the headlines now. *Strong Team Performance Due to Steroids—Not Prayer.*

"Gavin, stop it. I don't know anything for sure."

"What clued you in?"

"Mostly the changes in Brad and Joel and your comment about how much better the team has been doing. And this . . ." Jennie pulled a small piece of paper from under her note pad, then opened one of the large reference books to a place she'd marked.

"This is the note Courtney wrote to me. I've been so tuned in to to what she'd written I didn't pay that much attention to what she'd written the note on. I just figured since her dad was a pharmacist they had a lot of these scratch pads lying around. Anyway, I got to thinking maybe she used this particular pad for a reason."

"To let you know she was not only in trouble, but the kind of trouble she was in."

"Right. Dianabol is an anabolic steroid."

"Accusing the guys of taking 'roids is heavy stuff, Mc-Grady. You telling the cops?"

"Not yet. I want to talk to Coach Haskell first. I could still be wrong about this, and if word leaked out it could hurt a lot of people."

"You think Haskell might be involved?"

Jennie gazed into Gavin's hazel eyes. His concern matched hers. "I don't know. I hope I'm wrong about this."

"Yeah. I know what you mean. So when are you planning on talking to the coach?"

Jennie glanced at her watch. "How long do the guys practice?"

"Until about four." Gavin removed his glasses and cleaned them on his shirttail. "I think I should go with you." He grasped the wire frames and set them back on his face.

"You look worried."

"I am—about you."

"Me?"

"Think about it, Jennie. Someone beat up Courtney. We don't know why. We've speculated that she may have cut off someone's drug supply, but she could have been beaten for something else—maybe threatening to expose the steroid users. If the police found out about it, it would mean the end of Trinity's football team. It could even mean the end of the sports program. Brad and Joel's careers would be ruined. There are a lot of people who wouldn't want that to happen. Joel's dad and Coach Haskell for sure. I could name others."

"Which means my suspect list isn't nearly long enough."

"Which means if you go on asking questions or even hint that you suspect the guys are using steroids, you could be next."

Jennie gathered up her papers and stuffed them into her black leather backpack.

Walking out of the library was like walking into a sauna. The clear, comfortably warm day had turned into a slightly overcast steam bath. They left Gavin's bike locked in the bike rack and drove back to the school. The guys were still scrimmaging.

Cassie occupied the space she had earlier and waved when she saw them. "Where's Lisa?" she called. "She okay?"

"She's taking a nap." Jennie trudged up the bleachers for the second time that day and plopped down beside Cassie. The climb had drained her. "How can they play so long in this heat? The sweat's dripping off me and we just walked in from the parking lot." Jennie used her arm to wipe the moisture from her forehead.

"It was great until about half an hour ago. Clouds moved in." Cassie removed her cap and peered at the gray sky. "We'll probably have a thunderstorm tonight."

Jennie nodded. She didn't want to talk about the weather. "Cassie? Do you know anything about steroids?"

Gavin winced and gave her a didn't-you-hear-a-word-I-said? look.

Cassie stared straight ahead, her body rigid as a marble statue. "Yeah. Some. I know it's bad stuff." Cassie turned slightly to face Jennie. "Why do you want to know?"

Jennie swallowed hard, wondering how much to say. "I think Courtney may have been supplying it to some of the guys on the team."

"You mean like Brad?"

And Joel, Jennie thought but didn't say it. "Maybe. Brad did meet Courtney the night she disappeared." Jennie pulled the note Courtney had written from her pocket. "I got to wondering about this drug so I looked it up."

"Coach," one of the players on the field yelled. "You'd better get over here quick. We got a man down."

The three spectators jumped to their feet at the same time. Jennie stuffed the note into the front pocket of her jeans and tried to focus on the guy lying spread-eagle on the grass.

Cassie gasped. "It's Joel. Something's wrong with Joel." She was at the bottom of the bleachers by the time she got the last word out. Jennie and Gavin followed. Jennie sprinted ahead and reached the players first, breaking through the huddle to get to Joel.

Coach Haskell hunkered down beside him, apparently checking for a pulse. "What happened here? I didn't see him get hit."

"He didn't," Brad offered. "He was staggering around

like he couldn't get his breath. Then he grabbed his gut and went down."

"One of you guys better call 9-1-1. I'm not getting a pulse."

18

"Joel!" Cassie screamed. "Oh no, how could this happen?"

"Stay back." Jennie stepped in front of her to keep her from getting in Coach Haskell's way. "Brad, hold on to her."

Coach Haskell tipped Joel's head back to get an airway and blew into his mouth. Joel's chest rose and fell.

The rest of the team stood there staring open-mouthed as though they'd never seen anyone do CPR before. Jennie whacked Leif Hanson, the guy standing closest to her, on the back. "You heard the coach. Call 9–1–1. Move!"

Leif mumbled something and left.

To Gavin she said, "Maybe you'd better go with him. He looks pretty shook." Gavin nodded and sprinted after Leif.

"McGrady? That you?" the coach asked as he stopped the breathing and moved to Joel's chest to start compressions.

"Yeah." Jennie knelt beside Joel's still body, ready to give assistance.

"Good. Three—four. Stand by. I may need you to relieve me."

A few minutes later, Coach Haskell signaled Jennie to take over for him. Jennie kept up the lifesaving rhythm until the paramedics arrived.

As she watched the ambulance drive away with Joel and

his sister inside, Jennie's arms and legs turned to Jell-O.

Coach Haskell put a hand on her shoulder. "Thanks for your help, McGrady. I wish more kids had CPR training. If you hadn't been here, I'm not sure I could have kept going. I got arthritis in my wrist and shoulders. . . . By the way, why are you here? I know it isn't because you love football." The creases in his face shifted into a warm smile.

"I wanted to talk to you, but . . ." Jennie glanced behind the coach to the twenty or so guys still glued to the field.

Haskell followed her gaze and blew his whistle. "What are you guys standing around for?" he yelled. "Hit the showers." They scattered like mice at a cat convention.

"They're pretty upset. Can't say as I blame them." He lifted his Miami Dolphins cap and brushed his thinning hair back. "You said you wanted to talk."

Jennie quickly shared her suspicions with the coach. His dark bushy eyebrows nearly came together as he frowned. "These are serious allegations, Jennie. You said Brad denies using anything."

"Yes, but . . ."

"And you don't know for sure that Courtney was dispensing drugs."

"No, but . . ."

"Then we have to give him the benefit of the doubt."

"But the symptoms. Joel and Brad have gotten huge and more aggressive. And just now with Joel. The stuff I read said steroid use could cause a person to have a heart attack."

"Jennie, listen. If Joel had a heart attack, and I doubt that's the case, it sure wasn't from using steroids. They're good boys. I watch them real close—even do drug screening every now and then to make sure."

Jennie opened her mouth to argue her case, but Coach Haskell held up a hand to silence her. "I can understand why you'd be concerned. They are bigger and more aggressive, but that's from the special training programs Buck and I have been putting them through. If they're getting rough with their girlfriends, then I'll have a talk with them. My boys have been training hard. They're growing up. And something else too, Jennie. All these years I've been praying—asking God for a strong healthy team." He raised his hands and glanced upward. "And I thank the Lord, He's finally come through. Now if you really want to be helpful, you'll start praying for Joel's recovery instead of spreading gossip about this steroid business. The only hormone in these guys is testosterone— the kind that comes naturally at their age.

"Now," he added, dismissing her, "I need to get back to the locker room and calm my boys down. Then I'll head over to the hospital."

"I'm going to the hospital too," Jennie said. "I guess I'll see you there."

"Now, Jennie," he said, placing a hand on her shoulder, "I want you to forget this nonsense. Whatever you do, don't go making any trouble for Joel and his family—or Brad either. You haven't told the police, have you?"

"No, I wanted to verify it first."

"Good. That's good. Tell you what, McGrady. I appreciate your concern and I promise I'll keep an eye out. In fact, I haven't tested for drug use in a while. I'll do that."

She offered him a half smile. At least he hadn't totally discounted her.

———

Jennie dropped Gavin off at the library to get his bike, then hurried home to shower and change. She briefly filled her mother in on Joel's collapse before leaving for the hospital.

"They have no idea what's wrong?" Mom asked as she accompanied Jennie to the front porch.

Jennie had an idea, but didn't voice it. "I'll call as soon as I find out anything."

"Why do I get the feeling you're holding something back?"

"Maybe because I am." Jennie leaned against the porch railing and hoisted herself up. "I guess it would be okay to tell you." She paused again, hoping she was doing the right thing. "I think Courtney may have been supplying Joel and Brad and maybe some of the other guys with steroids. I was reading about steroid use today, and both Brad and Joel fit the description of someone who's been on them for a while. That's why I asked you about them earlier. I talked to Coach Haskell, but he denies it."

Mom rubbed her forehead and sighed. "You may be right. I went back over Frank's invoices and statements. There were several that didn't balance with what he showed on his inventory. Two different drug companies billed Frank for merchandise he apparently never received.

"Steroids?" Jennie asked.

Mom nodded. "In both cases the company had shipped Dianabol. It looks as though Courtney may have placed the orders, taken the merchandise without ever putting it into inventory, then destroyed the invoices so Frank wouldn't know what had been ordered. Since she did a lot of the bookkeeping, she just made out the checks for Frank to sign."

Jennie hopped off the railing. She had the evidence she needed. It was time to talk to the police. "Mom, do me a favor and call Rocky. Give him the information about Joel and tell him to meet me at the hospital. Better call Michael too—I have a feeling that family and Coach Haskell are going to need a lot of prayer."

———

Jennie walked into the waiting room just off the large double doors labeled emergency. Cassie was sitting alone in a pale blue chair near the receptionist's desk. She glanced up from the magazine she'd been reading when Jennie slumped into the chair across from her.

"The doctor thinks Joel's had a heart attack." Cassie's voice held no hint of the fear Jennie had seen in her earlier. Now she seemed as composed as ever. "Which is impossible," she went on. "Joel's heart is perfect. He's in better shape than he's ever been in."

It's one of the side effects of steroid use. Jennie didn't express her opinion aloud. It didn't seem appropriate to make those kind of allegations right now. She'd wait for Rocky and Michael.

"I wish Dad and Mom would get here. Maybe the doctor will listen to them. They'll insist on another opinion."

A youngish man in green surgical scrubs and eyes that matched came through the ER doors. "Miss Nielsen," he said. "Your parents haven't arrived yet, I see." He glanced at Jennie. "Are you family?"

"No, I'm . . ." Jennie started to say friend, but that wasn't exactly right either.

"Her name is Jennie McGrady. She's the one who helped Coach Haskell with the CPR."

"I'm Doctor Clark." He stretched his hand in Jennie's direction. "I've heard about you."

Jennie grasped it. "Is Joel going to be okay? Cassie said you thought he had a heart attack."

"Yes. It certainly looks that way." His lean build and the way he wore his ash blond hair reminded her of Ryan. He turned back to Cassie. "Has your brother ever had seizures?"

"No." Cassie's eyes widened with the same fear Jennie had seen in them earlier. "Why?"

"He had one a few minutes ago. He's stable now. We're waiting for some blood work. Did your parents give you any indication when they might arrive?"

Cassie shook her head. "They both work at Nike. They're probably stuck in traffic."

Dr. Clark examined his watch. "Let the receptionist know the minute they arrive. Miss McGrady," he went on, his gaze drifting to Jennie again. "I'm glad you're here. Would you mind coming with me for a moment? I'd like to ask you a few questions about Joel's condition before the ambulance arrived."

"Sure." Jennie followed him through the doors and into a small office. She wondered which of the closed curtains Joel was behind.

He pointed to a chair, then instead of sitting in the one behind the desk, pulled a rolling stool from the next room and sat on it. "Now then, what can you tell me?"

Jennie opened her mouth, then closed it again.

"It's okay. I don't expect a professional opinion. Just tell me what you saw."

"Not that much, really." Jennie went back over the scene and told him what Brad and some of the others had told her.

He jotted down some notes. "How long did you administer CPR?"

"About fifteen minutes. Coach Haskell took the first seven, then I relieved him. You don't think there'll be any brain damage, do you?"

"I don't know. He did have a seizure. We're trying to determine a cause."

Steroids. The word screamed into Jennie's mind. Jennie stared at her hands. "Dr. Clark. Umm, there's something you should know about Joel. I . . . I don't know for sure, but I think he might be taking Dianabol."

Dr. Clark raised an eyebrow, but didn't seem surprised. He glanced over Jennie's head and spoke to someone behind her. "Can I help you?"

"Dean Rockford," a familiar voice said. "Police."

Rocky.

"I believe this young lady has some information that might be of interest to both of us," he said. "Mind if I sit in?"

Without waiting for an invitation, Rocky hooked a chair and dragged it into the cubicle. They were seated perfectly for three-cornered catch and Jennie wondered what they'd do with the information she was about to pitch to them.

After a brief explanation of what Rocky was doing there, Jennie launched into her story. It should have gotten easier with the telling, but the heartbreak of kids killing themselves to win a game made the possibility more and more difficult to accept.

When she'd finished, she felt drained. Doctor Clark made a teepee with his hands and rested his chin on the tips of his fingers. She almost expected him to say "v-e-r-r-y interesting." But he didn't. After a moment, he got up, thanked her for her help, and walked across the wide hall to the nurses station.

Rocky looked at her and shook his head.

"You don't believe me? You think I'm making this up?"

"Oh, I believe you, Jennie. I'm just trying to figure out what you think you're doing. You've known about this homeless girl for how long? Why am I hearing about all this for the first time today?"

Dr. Clark appeared again and nodded at Rocky. "Could I talk to you privately?" To Jennie he said, "You might be more comfortable in the waiting room."

Rocky walked with the doctor across the hall where they conversed in tones too low for her to hear. Jennie chewed on her lower lip, stretched her long legs out in front of her and crossed them. *Maybe you shouldn't have said anything, McGrady. What if you're wrong?*

19

"I am right," she murmured under her breath.

Jennie decided to take Dr. Clark's advice and made her way back down the hall and through the double doors, nearly colliding with the receptionist.

Once in the waiting room, she almost turned around and went back. Joel's parents had arrived and looked up at her expectantly. Cassie glared at her for a moment, then looked away. *She knows, McGrady. She knows you told them about the steroids.* Coach Haskell took a step toward her, then stopped. He probably knew too.

Michael, who'd most likely been consoling them, smiled at her. Only it was a surface smile. Underneath she could feel his uneasiness—nearly as strongly as she felt her own.

Had she made the wrong choice in revealing her suspicions? Using steroids was illegal—and dangerous. No. She'd done the right thing. So why did she feel so rotten?

"You must be Jennie." Mr. Nielsen, a tall angular man with narrow hips and wide shoulders, rose and walked toward her. His eyes were the same brown color as Joel and Cassie's. "Cassie was just telling us how you and Coach Haskell saved Joel's life. We're very grateful. Did they . . . did the doctor tell you anything?"

Jennie shook her head. "No, he just had some questions."

Dr. Clark emerged from the ER, his face somber. "Mr.

and Mrs. Nielsen. Good, you're here. Would you mind coming with me for a few minutes? I need you to sign some papers and . . ."

"The papers can wait," Nielsen growled. "How's my son? What's all this nonsense about a heart attack?"

"That's what I'd like to discuss." The doctor took a step back, obviously intimidated by Nielsen's size and fierceness. Like father, like son.

"Well, discuss it then," Nielsen shot back. "Whatever you have to say, you can say right here. I'd prefer having some witnesses around to confirm your misdiagnosis."

Dr. Clark glanced around and shrugged. "I know it's difficult to believe, but Joel did suffer a heart attack. And shortly after he arrived here he had a seizure."

"But he's so young!" Mrs. Nielsen spoke this time. "How could something like this happen?"

"There are a number of reasons." The doctor drew in a deep breath. "Mr. and Mrs. Nielsen, were you aware that your son was using steroids?"

Mr. Nielsen exploded. Mrs. Nielsen cried. Cassie glared at Jennie as though the entire incident had been her fault. Coach Haskell tossed Jennie a look of disbelief, then sank into a chair and stared at a muted brown, blue, and green weaving that hung on the far wall.

"You'll be hearing from my lawyer," Nielsen threatened when he ran out of expletives. Or maybe he just remembered that Michael was in the room.

"Buck, please." His wife stepped between the two men. "Dr. Clark. I don't understand any of this."

"Heart attacks in young men are rare. That along with his muscle mass led me to run a blood test to determine whether or not he'd been using steroids. The test came out positive."

Jennie had been right. But the knowledge didn't cheer her. Feeling more like a traitor than a hero, she left Joel's family and Coach Haskell in Michael's capable hands and wandered out into the hospital corridor.

Since the ambulance had taken Joel to the same hospital Courtney was in, Jennie decided to see how she was doing. First, though, she needed something to eat. In the cafeteria, she indulged herself with a Coke and a rich, gooey chocolate brownie. Probably the farthest you could get from health food. Which was fine with Jennie. She'd had it with the body beautiful crowd.

After tossing her trash in the garbage can, Jennie climbed the stairs to the fourth floor. The expected grip of panic didn't come. Instead she felt an overwhelming sense of sadness. For Joel and Brad—for the school and for far too many people to name. Each set of stairs brought a name to her lips and a prayer to her heart.

Jennie checked in at the nurses station before going to Courtney's room.

"She's a little better," the nurse told her. "We've upgraded her condition from critical to serious."

"She's still not out of the coma?"

"No, she's not. But we're hopeful."

Jennie thanked her and moved away from the desk. The sign on the door still forbade visitors. As she'd done before, Jennie stood outside the room and watched Courtney through the large window. She looked the same—pale and lifeless.

She heard voices down the hall and turned toward them. Gavin was there, probably getting the same report she had. He walked toward her.

Jennie wondered for a moment if Gavin might have been on steroids as well. He'd have been a likely candidate. She remembered their conversation about jocks getting the girls and Gavin's bitterness toward Courtney for dropping him. He hadn't developed any muscle that she could see. *You're getting paranoid, McGrady. Totally paranoid.*

She thought about mentioning the possibility to Rocky. Only she didn't want to. If the police wanted to know who else was involved in Courtney's drug dealings they could find out on their own.

"Think she's gonna make it?" Gavin said as he joined Jennie at the window.

"How would I know?" The words sounded harsher than she'd intended. She looked at their nearly identical shapes reflected in the window. The sight did not please her.

He frowned as he glanced at her, probably wondering what he'd done to deserve her anger.

"I'm sorry," Jennie said. "I shouldn't be taking it out on you."

Gavin shrugged and to her reflection said, "I can understand why you'd be upset. I stopped by the emergency room on my way up here. Nielsen is furious. He's threatening to sue the hospital, the school, the coach, and Mr. Evans. And you."

"Me?"

"Cassie told him you instigated the investigation."

"That's stupid. The doctor didn't need my input. He already knew."

"Well, don't feel bad. He'll probably sue me too when he reads the morning paper."

Jennie turned from their reflections to look at the real Gavin. "You've already done an article?"

"Yeah. All I need is your side of it." Gavin met her eyes for a moment, then looked away. "I'm not going to apologize, Jennie. If I'm going to make it as a reporter I have to be tough."

"When did you have time? I just left the ER twenty minutes ago."

"After you dropped me off at the house, I went to see Brad. I told him we knew about the steroids. At first he argued with me, but when I told him some of the side effects, and that Joel had had a heart attack, he buckled. Got real scared. Told me he and Joel started using the stuff about the same time Joel started dating Courtney."

"Did he say why?"

Gavin shrugged. "Only that Joel talked him into using it."

Jennie's heart felt like a lead weight. "They must have known how dangerous steroids can be."

"They knew it was bad stuff, but figured taking them for a year or two wouldn't be a big deal. They were only going to do it until they graduated."

"Did he confess to beating up Courtney?"

"No. He only admits to meeting her. She told him she didn't know how much longer she could supply the stuff. Her dad was getting suspicious. That's all he claims to know. Says he's glad things are out in the open."

Jennie turned around and leaned back against the window. "All we've managed to do is determine that Courtney was guilty of supplying drugs. We still don't know who wanted her dead."

Gavin moved up beside her, rested his knuckles on the windowsill, and let his forehead touch the glass. Jennie followed his gaze to the slender figure lying bruised and battered on the bed. "You're right about that," he said in a voice so quiet she could barely hear him. He pushed away from the wall again. "I'm a pretty good judge of character and I think Brad was telling the truth."

"Hmmm. I think he is too. I mean . . . since Courtney was their supplier, it makes no sense that he'd try to kill her."

Jennie felt like a player in a board game. She'd nearly completed the course then had gotten a card telling her to go back to square one.

"Why worry about it?" Gavin said. "I talked to your friend Rocky while I was upstairs. He says the D.A.'s got a solid case against Frank Evans."

"They did before."

"Yeah, well, my mom's been keeping really close tabs on the case. She says the blood and hair samples they found in the trunk of Evans' car definitely match Courtney's."

Jennie uncrossed her ankles and pushed herself away from the wall. "So I guess I was wrong in thinking it may have been someone else."

"I guess so." Gavin clasped her shoulder. "Hey, we can't be right all the time. Besides, you gotta let the police solve a case once in a while or they'd feel bad."

That brought a smile to Jennie's face. "Very funny."

"Listen, I gotta go finish my article." He started to leave then turned around again. "Um . . . how about doing me a favor? I'm heading over to *The Oregonian*—be there for a couple of hours. Could you pick me up later and take me out to the farm?"

"Sure—if you do me a favor."

He grinned. "Why do I get the feeling I'm being manipulated? Okay, I'll bite. What?"

"Don't say anything about me in your article. You really don't have to. The doctor's the one who found steroids in Joel's bloodstream. The police were already looking into the drug thing. Even if I hadn't done anything, the truth would have come out—eventually."

"You don't give yourself enough credit, Jen." Gavin smiled and left without giving her an answer.

Jennie watched him go. They were a lot alike, not just in physical stature, but mentally too. They both had an investigative bent and a desire to find the truth.

The truth. Jennie looked at Courtney again. Would they ever know what really happened to the girl with the rainbow hair?

Had her own father beat her up and left her for dead? Could this seemingly kind man, a man her mother was working for and dating, be a murderer? Jennie shivered. "Oh, Courtney," she whispered. "Please wake up. You're the only one who can tell us what really happened."

One of the monitors at the nurses' station switched from a rhythmic beep to a long dull tone. Jennie knew the sound. It meant someone on the unit may have gone into cardiac arrest.

"Excuse us, miss." Two nurses hurried into Courtney's room. They stood on either side of her bed, apparently checking her vital signs.

As Jennie watched, dread crept in and through her like maggots on a dead possum. *Don't die, Courtney. Please don't die.*

20

Jennie slowly opened her eyes.

The nurses hovered over Courtney, but they weren't acting like they had an emergency on their hands. One of the nurses flipped a switch on the panel at the head of the bed.

The respirator stopped pumping air into Courtney's lungs. Jennie stared at the still figure on the bed until tears blurred her vision.

Moments later she felt a hand on her shoulder. "Is something wrong?" It was the nurse who'd pulled the plug.

"Is she dead?" Jennie asked.

"Oh, goodness no. You mean because we disconnected the respirator? No. She's fine. We've been weaning her off and she's breathing on her own now."

"But the monitor . . ."

The nurse smiled. "You're very observant. Actually, one of the lines connected to the heart monitor came loose. We reattached it."

"So Courtney's getting better?"

"In some ways, yes. She's still in a coma and we have no way of knowing how long that will last. But, if she continues to make this kind of progress we'll be moving her out of intensive care as early as tomorrow."

Before heading home, Jennie decided to check on Joel. He'd been transferred to the coronary care unit on the second floor. Before going up, she stopped at a row of pay phones near the hospital entrance and called her mom again. The answering machine picked up. Jennie left a message letting Mom know where she was and hung up.

The Nielsens seemed much more subdued than when she'd seen them earlier. Maybe Michael had calmed them down. He was good at that. "I just came by to see how Joel was doing," she said, trying to sound cheerful, but not too much so.

"That was very sweet of you, dear," Mrs. Nielsen said. "Joel had another seizure."

Michael rose and walked toward Jennie. He placed an arm around her shoulders. "You look exhausted."

"I'm fine. Just a little tired. It seems like everyone I know is ending up in the hospital. Lisa. Courtney. Joel. It's scary." Jennie smiled up at him. "I have some good news, though."

"Oh yeah? And what might that be?"

"Courtney's off the respirator. She's definitely getting better."

"Really?" Cassie said, acknowledging Jennie's presence for the first time. "That's great." She glanced at the floor, then back up at Jennie. "I'm glad you came back. There's something I wanted to tell you. Um . . . do you want to go have a Coke or something?"

Jennie wanted to go home and have dinner. The sugar from the gooey chocolate bar had long since disappeared from her bloodstream. She also wanted to hear what Cassie had to say.

"Cassie. Wait a second," Mr. Nielsen said, digging into the hip pocket of his dark gray slacks and extracting his billfold. "Why don't you take Jennie down to the cafeteria and get some dinner. I think it's the least we can do." He handed a twenty to Cassie and she stuffed it in the front pocket of her powder blue cutoffs.

Jennie started to object, but when her stomach growled in protest, she acquiesced. Sometimes you just had to follow a higher calling.

"I owe you an apology," Cassie said while they waited for the elevator. I wasn't very nice to you earlier. I guess I felt like I had to blame somebody and you . . ."

"It's okay, really. You must have been really scared, seeing Joel go down like that."

"I was. To be honest, Jennie, when we were sitting in the stands and you asked if I knew anything about steroids I about panicked."

The elevator doors swooshed open. They waited for an orderly to push out an empty wheelchair, then stepped inside. Cassie pushed the "G" button and waited until the doors closed before she continued.

"I didn't know they were using 'roids until after Courtney disappeared. Then I overheard Brad and Joel talking. They were trying to figure out a way to get more when their supply ran out. I was so mad."

The elevator released them on the ground floor. Jennie and Cassie both passed on the cafeteria special—cheese enchiladas that looked like they'd already been through someone's digestive system. Instead they opted for the salad bar.

They found an unoccupied table along the far wall and sat down. Cassie speared a plump red strawberry and popped it into her mouth. Jennie started in on her garden salad, deciding to save the fruit for dessert.

"I know what you're thinking," Cassie said. "You're wondering why I didn't tell anyone. I guess for the same reason no one else did. I didn't want to ruin Joel's chances for a football career—Brad's either, but Joel was my main concern." She broke off a piece of bread and began buttering it. "See, it wasn't just Joel. I knew if my dad found out, it would destroy him. Well, you saw him. Dad's dream has been for Joel to get picked up by a major team. Dad's been grooming him since he was born."

"What's going to happen now?"

"I don't know. Once this gets out, Joel will be finished in sports. Dad might lose his endorsements. Mom says it will all work out and the most important thing now is for Joel to get well. I hope she's right." Cassie set her knife on the tray. The sadness in her deep brown eyes almost made Jennie cry.

Her sigh seemed to come from her toes. "Oh, Jennie. If I'd known where all this would lead, I'd have told Mom and Dad when I first suspected." A fat tear dripped down her tan cheek. She brushed it away with the back of her hand. "I'd have found some way to make them stop."

Jennie didn't know what to say or how to console her. The saddest part about their tragedy was that it could have been prevented.

Then something Cassie had said popped to the surface of Jennie's brain like a huge zit. "You said 'for the same reason no one else did.' You mean someone else knew? Like the coach?"

"No. Coach Haskell didn't suspect a thing. He did routine urine tests on the players. Joel and Brad had worked out this scam with a couple of the other guys. They switched containers."

"Why would anyone go along with them?"

"For the good of the team." Cassie heaved an exasperated sigh. "You just don't get it, do you, McGrady? Brad and Joel are the biggest guys on the team. Without them Trinity doesn't have a chance."

"So they justified breaking the law. You're right, Cassie, I don't get it. I know sports is important to a lot of people. I love swimming and going to games. When my dad was home, I used to hang out with him on weekends and watch the bowl games and the Olympics. But . . . I don't know. I might put my life on the line to save someone if I had to, but I'd never risk my life to win a game."

They ate in silence for a few minutes before Cassie spoke again. "You said Courtney's getting better . . . I'm glad. I mean, Courtney shouldn't have been supplying drugs but she didn't deserve to get beat up like that. Is she still in a coma?"

"Yes." Jennie sighed, glad for the change in subject. "The nurse told me she could wake up any time—or she might not wake up for years."

"Isn't there any way they can tell?"

"I guess not. We'll just have to wait and see."

Jennie left the hospital in a much better mood. Courtney was going to be okay. Even though the nurse had warned her against being overly optimistic, Jennie refused to think anything but positive thoughts about Courtney's condition.

She felt better about Joel too—though she hadn't been able to see him, his condition had been upgraded to serious by the time she and Cassie got back from dinner.

And poor Cassie. What a dilemma she'd been in. Jennie could understand why Cassie hadn't told anyone about the steroids. There had been so much at stake.

Jennie wished she hadn't agreed to meet Gavin. She felt like she'd been on a forty-eight-hour marathon and all she really wanted to do was sleep. The case was closed. Police had a suspect in Courtney's assault and Jennie had uncovered the steroid scandal.

But she couldn't go home just yet; she'd made a promise. When she pulled up in front of *The Oregonian* offices, Gavin was waiting outside. They secured his bike in her trunk and headed for the country. On the way, Jennie filled him in on Courtney's condition and her own encounter with the Nielsens.

When Jennie asked about the article, he pulled a folder

out of his pack and read it to her. When he'd finished he asked, "Well, what do you think?"

"You didn't mention me."

"You asked me not to."

"I know." Jennie flashed him a grin. "I just didn't think you'd do it. Thanks."

"You're welcome. So, how was it?"

"Good. Really good. I like the way you make your points without sounding judgmental. And that part about Courtney—a soft heart that went too far."

"She was wrong to give people drugs," Gavin admitted. "But I think in her own way she wanted to help. Like giving Tina the insulin. I keep wondering what I would have done. I mean . . . do you walk away and let someone die because they refuse to go to a doctor?"

"That would be such a hard decision."

"The part I have the hardest time with is the steroids." Gavin frowned. "How could she have agreed to supply Brad and Joel with that stuff?"

"How could she have picked him over me?" Gavin hadn't asked the question out loud but his expression left little doubt in Jennie's mind what he was thinking. Gavin's anger filled the car with an almost tangible aura. He stared straight ahead as sullen and still as the moments before a storm.

Tension knotted itself around her. She wanted to console him—to reassure him, but didn't know how.

By the time Jennie pulled into his driveway, Gavin had pulled himself together and was telling her about his plans for college.

Once Jennie got to the farm, she didn't want to leave—at least not right away. She loved being out in the open, away from buildings and the smog of the city. "I have relatives that own a ranch in Montana," Jennie said as the thought came to her. "Being out here reminded me. I wonder how they're doing?"

Gavin gave her a strange look. "You don't know?"

"Not really. Maggie—that's my mom's older sister—doesn't correspond much. About the only time we hear from them is Christmas. Last Christmas we got this picture of her family in front of some llamas. She didn't say much except that they were starting a new life in the Bitterroot Valley in Montana."

"Hmmm." Gavin stared into the field.

"Where's your mother?" Jennie asked, changing the subject.

"At class. She teaches writing at Portland State. Ummm—I have some chores to do before it gets dark. Want to help?"

"Sure." Jennie pulled on a pair of Maddie's rubber boots and slogged through the pasture and barn behind Gavin, feeding the llamas and goats. At nine-fifteen, Jennie firmly announced that she had to get home.

She'd tried calling her mother a couple times but no one had answered. Now she was getting worried. She'd just opened her car door when Maddie pulled in.

"Jennie, I'm glad you're here." If smiles were light bulbs, Maddie's would have lit up the entire yard.

"Hi, Mrs. Winslow." Jennie closed the door of her Mustang to turn off the door-open ding.

"Have you thought about the book?" Maddie asked. "I have wonderful news. I talked to my agent yesterday and she's thrilled. All we need is an okay from you and she'll start pursuing contracts for the book and a movie."

"Movie?" Jennie's heart did a triple flip. "Are you serious?"

"Absolutely. Oh, I know you'll need to talk to your mother, but I really hope this works out. It could be my big break—and yours too, Jennie."

"I wouldn't get my hopes up," Gavin interjected. "I mean

. . . your story would make a great novel, but Mom tends to overreact."

"Gavin." Maddie tossed him a disgruntled look. "Don't pay any attention to him, Jennie—he's picked up his father's practical bent. He's right, of course, there's a possibility it won't sell, but like I always tell my students, failure isn't determined by how often you fail. You only fail when you stop trying."

Maddie's enthusiasm spread over Jennie like infectious laughter. How could she say no? "I'll talk to my mom about it. I have to warn you, though, she's extremely practical."

"Would you like me to come by? It might help if your mother and I got better acquainted. I know if it were Gavin, I'd want to know all the details and be in on the plans."

"That'd be great. I'll call you. In the meantime, I'd better hustle. If I don't get home before eleven, Mom's liable to make good on her threat to lock me up until I'm twenty-one."

Maddie gave her a knowing wink. "I think your mother and I are going to get along just fine." Her face clouded over. "Speaking of your mother . . . have you heard the news at all today?"

"No, why?" Her stomach tightened as if preparing itself to expect the worst.

"Remember the other day when you were here and I was going on about how inadequate our judicial system is?"

Jennie nodded.

"Well, they did it up big this time. With all the evidence against him, they let him go. Frank Evans is out on bail."

21

"What are they thinking?" Maddie rolled her eyes. "We have more criminals out on the street these days than in prison."

"But what about the evidence against him?" Gavin asked, echoing Jennie's thoughts.

"Apparently, they feel aggravated assault isn't a serious enough charge." She threw up her hands. "I don't know why I let things like this get to me. I should be used to it by now. Even if he does go to trial and is found guilty, he probably won't get more than a slap on the wrist."

Maddie took a deep breath and let it out slowly. "I'm sorry, kids. I really shouldn't go on like that. It's just that sometimes it seems like our judicial system does little more than protect the criminal. I just hope the police think to post a guard outside Courtney's room. If he's guilty, he may try again."

"I'm sure they will, Mrs. Winslow." Jennie grasped the door handle of her Mustang. "I . . . I really have to go. It's getting late."

Jennie left feeling a bit overwhelmed and helpless. Some things were just too big to fight. *They let Frank Evans out on bail. What if he's guilty?* The thought exploded in her brain again and again. She had to get home. Courtney's safety concerned her, but someone else's safety occupied her thoughts even more. Mom. Did Mom know he was out? Did she still believe in his innocence?

"Please, God, keep her safe." Jennie repeated the prayer a dozen times on her way home.

The moment she turned from Elm onto Magnolia and saw the dark house, Jennie knew something was wrong. *What if he's guilty?* Her blood pounded the question out in rhythm through her veins. Until the courts proved otherwise, Frank Evans was a threat, whether Mom believed it or not.

She took several deep breaths and let them out slowly to calm her frayed nerves. Once parked and out of the car, Jennie raced up the walk and onto the porch. The door was locked. She let herself in.

"Mom?" Jennie yelled. The silence penetrated her heart like a knife.

What if he's guilty? A dim light from the kitchen drew her toward it. Mom had left the stove light on and a note on the table.

> *Jennie,*
> *Nick and Hannah are spending the night at Kevin and Kate's. I've gone with Frank to the pharmacy to help him sort out the inventory problem we talked about. The way it looks, I'll be there until at least midnight. Call me when you get home.*
> *Love you, Mom*

Jennie didn't like it. She grabbed the phone and punched in the numbers Mom had jotted down on the note. The clock on the microwave read ten-fifteen. After six rings, Frank finally picked up. "Hello."

"Hi, can I . . ."

". . . this is Evans' Pharmacy. I'm sorry we missed your call. Our hours are . . ."

The answering machine. Jennie slammed down the receiver. Maybe Mom was on her way home. *What if he's guilty?*

Jennie tried to push the unwanted thought away, but it clung to her like a wet T-shirt. Though the night was a balmy seventy degrees, goose bumps raised the hair on her arms and sent shivers through her body. She took several deep breaths. *Steady, McGrady. Mom's fine. She could be on her way home. Or maybe they went out for a snack or coffee.*

Okay, now what? She could call the police and have them check things out. Only that might upset Mom. Apparently she still believed in Frank's innocence or she'd never have agreed to go with him.

Jennie swallowed hard to settle the panic rising in her chest. She picked up the receiver and dialed 9–1–1. Okay. Maybe she was overreacting, but she couldn't ignore the gut feeling that Mom was in trouble.

After reporting her concerns to the 9–1–1 operator, Jennie sat down to wait. That lasted about two seconds. On her feet again, she paced back and forth a few dozen times, then wandered out of the kitchen, through the dining room, and into the living room. She plopped down on the couch, picked up the remote control, turned the television on, then off again. The last thing she needed was more bad news. She popped back up again. "I'm going down there," she announced to the blank television screen.

Jennie dug the keys out of her jeans pocket and headed out the door. On the ten-minute drive to the pharmacy, she turned on the radio and cranked the volume up to drown out the negative thoughts that kept forming in her mind. When that didn't work she just kept telling herself, *Mom's okay. She is. God, please—let her be okay.*

Jennie parked in front of the store. A *closed* sign hung in the metal-framed glass door. Black wrought-iron security bars protected the door and display windows from potential thieves. *But not from the pharmacist himself,* she mused. Jennie glanced around. No sign of a police car. Maybe they'd already checked the place.

Everything looked peaceful, but Jennie still couldn't get over the feeling that something was wrong. Suddenly, the store lit up. Light poured out of the windows and onto the sidewalk. Jennie heaved a sigh of relief. Maybe she'd guessed right. They'd gone out for coffee and were just now coming back. They must have used a back entrance.

She stepped out of the car and pounded on the door. "Mom! Frank! It's me, Jennie. I . . ."

The door moved beneath the pressure of her hand. Jennie pushed harder and it opened. It should have been locked. She released the breath she'd been holding and entered the store.

The lights, she realized, weren't the daytime kind, but the subdued type used at night to allow the police to see inside the stores when they patrolled a neighborhood. It allowed her to see, but not all that well.

Somewhere in the distance she heard a motor roar to life and the screeching of tires. Her mind raced as fast as her heart as it tried to take in her surroundings. All kinds of miscellaneous products and medical supplies lined the well-stocked shelves. Everything neatly labeled and in its place. A few steps more and Jennie's heart stopped. The area behind the counter, where pharmacists shelved prescription drugs, had been ransacked.

Quiet. It was too quiet.

"Mom!" she called, breaking the deadly silence with the sound of her own voice. "Frank?" Jennie felt as though someone had wrapped a tourniquet around her stomach and twisted it tight.

She heard a shuffling sound off to her right. Someone groaned. Jennie wouldn't have thought it possible, but her stomach tightened even more. She was beginning to feel lightheaded as she moved toward the sound. It had come from a room in the back of the store—probably the office.

Sucking in several deep breaths to steady herself, Jennie

moved into the darkened hallway. Her foot slipped in something wet. She reached out to catch herself. Her hand brushed against the wall as she dropped to her knees. The dark liquid oozed into her jeans. Blood?

Jennie swallowed hard. No. Not blood. A broken bottle of some kind of syrup lay on the floor a couple feet away.

Using the doorframe to steady herself, she stood up. That's when she saw the arm. A woman's hand and forearm lay on the floor, bathed in soft light. The rest of her body was obliterated by shadows.

No. McGrady, don't even think it. She reached inside the room and felt along the wall for a light switch. She found it. The white fluorescent light blinded her, but not enough. The woman lay on her stomach. A freckled arm disappeared into a creamy silk blouse splayed with strands of beautiful auburn hair.

22

"Mom . . . Oh no—no." Jennie knew the whimpering cries were coming from her own throat, but they seemed too far away to be real. Tears clouded the sight of her mother's body and bloody wound on the side of her head. Panic tore at her insides. She wanted to scream and run, but couldn't move. From somewhere deep inside the recesses of her memory, Jennie heard the calming voice of her CPR instructor: *No matter how terrible the trauma, put the victims needs above your own. Stay calm, McGrady. You know what to do. Check for a pulse.*

Jennie drew in a shuddering breath and obeyed. Her fingers felt numb and awkward against her mother's neck. One . . . two . . . three. The rhythm of her pulse was strong and steady. And she was still breathing. Jennie slowed her own breathing down again. She had to get help. And stop the bleeding.

After calling 9–1–1, Jennie knelt and turned her mother's limp body over so that she lay on her back, her head cradled in Jennie's arms. The silk cream blouse was splattered with blood. So far the only injury she could see was the open gash on her left temple. As near as Jennie could tell, the bleeding had already stopped.

"Hmmm." Mom groaned and lifted her arm.

Jennie grabbed her hand and squeezed it. "It's okay. I'm

here. The ambulance is on the way." Sirens she'd heard in the backgroud grew louder and louder and finally stopped. Red, blue, and white lights flashed on the wall in the hallway.

Mom's eyelids flickered open, her green eyes fearful and filling with tears. "Frank. . . ." She tried to sit up.

"Mom, please, lie still." Mom collapsed back against Jennie's lap.

Had Frank done this to her? Jennie wanted to ask, but didn't get the chance. Police swarmed in, then the paramedics. Once Jennie had supplied the information, she stepped aside and watched them transfer Mom to a stretcher.

"You did a fine job, Miss McGrady," an officer in a tan and brown uniform said. He placed an arm across her shoulders and led her out of the room. She tried to read his name tag but tears blurred her vision again.

Jennie sniffed, trying to hold back the torrent of emotions that threatened to wash her away.

"I'm Deputy Mosier," he said. "Any idea what happened here?"

Jennie's head was spinning. Her knees buckled. Mosier's strong hands grasped her under the arms and lowered her to the floor. He pressed her head down between her knees. "Take some deep breaths," Mosier instructed. "That's good."

Another officer's shiny black shoes and pressed brown slacks joined Mosier's. "She able to tell you anything?" he asked.

"Not yet. Poor kid. Coming in and finding her mother like that."

Mosier hunkered down beside her. "I know this is tough for you, but we need to ask you a few more questions. Are you up to it?"

"I think so." Jennie straightened. "My mom left a note saying she'd be here. She does the books. I called and no one answered and I got scared."

"So you came to check things out? You really should have called us, you know."

"I did. About ten-fifteen. I got here about twenty minutes later and I waited. No one came. I figured maybe someone already checked it out and left again."

"I doubt it. We've had a busy night. Big tanker jack-knifed up on the freeway. So what made you decide to go in?"

"The lights came on in the store and I thought Mom and Frank had gone for coffee or something and were just coming back." *Frank.* "He's responsible for this. He was released on bail and . . ."

"Whoa. Hold on, there." Mosier stopped writing. "Who's Frank?"

Jennie told him.

"Ain't it the way? Spend half our time dealing with guys that never should have been released. But what do you do?"

Jennie had no idea. Her head was beginning to clear. She needed to get away. To be with her mother. To think. "I'd like to go now."

Mosier gave her an understanding nod. "I'll come by the hospital—talk to you there. Hopefully your mother will have some answers for us. Did you want to go in the ambulance with her?"

"Yes . . . no. I have my car here."

"You sure you can drive? I can have someone—"

"No, I'll be okay."

A few minutes later she left the flashing lights behind and headed for the hospital.

By the time the receptionist had cleared Jennie to go into the emergency room, her mother had fully regained consciousness. A hospital gown had replaced the silk blouse. The gash in her forehead had been sutured shut, and a woman in scrubs and surgical gloves was lifting a rectangular piece of white gauze from a cloth-covered tray. "Hi. I'm Doctor Martin. You must be this lady's missing daughter."

"Jennie, honey." Mom held out a bloodstained hand. Jennie gripped it, surprised at her mother's strength. "I was getting worried."

"You were worried about me?" Jennie shook her head. "In case you hadn't noticed, you're the one getting stitches. Parents." She gave the doctor an exasperated look. "Can't leave them alone for a minute."

"Gives you a lot of trouble, does she?" Dr. Martin smiled.

Jennie and her mother both answered in the affirmative.

"That's it." Dr. Martin applied the last piece of tape across the bandage.

"Am I ready to go?" Mom asked.

"Not quite. I'd like to keep you a bit longer, just to be sure. You've got a nasty bump."

Mom sighed. "I'm fine, really."

"Then you won't mind answering some questions." Deputy Mosier stepped around the curtains and introduced himself.

Mom looked down at her unflattering attire and shrugged. "Why not. I'm not sure I'll be of any help."

"Just tell me what happened."

Mom closed her eyes. "I went with Frank to the pharmacy to verify some discrepancies I'd found in his books. We got there about eight. At around ten, Frank wanted to take a break. I wasn't at a place where I could stop, so I sent him out to get coffee and donuts."

"When did he get back?"

"He didn't." She glanced up at Jennie. Deep furrows lined her forehead. "You don't think he did this?"

"Who else would have?" Jennie asked. "Frank was out on bail. He . . ."

"No. It wasn't him." Mom raked her fingers through her hair. "I thought I heard him come in, but when I called out to him, no one answered. Then the lights went out. I got up. Someone came into the room and . . ." She touched her forehead. "Whoever it was shoved me down. I must have hit my head on the desk.

"But it wasn't Frank. The person who pushed me was smaller. Tall, but slender—younger." Mom's eyes widened. "Frank. He must be frantic. We need to find him."

"We've already done that, ma'am. He came in a few minutes after you left." Mosier's eyes narrowed. "He's been taken downtown for questioning. Says he got stuck in traffic—which may be true. Accident up on I–205 had traffic blocked for a couple of hours."

"Oh, that poor man. After all he's been through and then to have his store burglarized."

"That poor man?" Jennie was losing it. She couldn't understand how her mother could so adamantly defend a man everyone else thought was guilty. "Did you ever stop to think that all of this stuff might be happening because he's guilty?"

"Jennie, please. Lower your voice."

Jennie clamped her teeth together. She folded her arms and sank into a chair near the wall. How could Mom be so blind?

Jennie tuned out Mom and Mosier and thought back to the scene she'd encountered at the pharmacy. She'd been quick to name Frank as the suspect. Now that she thought about it, several questions surfaced. First, why would he burglarize his own store? And why take Mom to the store if he was going to hurt her? That didn't make much sense.

She glanced over at her mom who was still adamantly defending Evans. *Okay, McGrady, admit it. You jumped the gun. You let yourself get so worked up when you heard Frank was out on bail that you put your brain in neutral.*

Jennie unclenched her jaw, unfolded her arms, and went back to her mom's side. "I'm sorry I got mad."

Mom took hold of her hand and squeezed it.

"I . . . I think I'll go up and see how Courtney is doing," Jennie said. "I'll be back in half an hour or so."

"That sounds like a wonderful idea. Hopefully they'll be ready to let me go by then."

Jennie's spirits lifted some when the nurse told her Courtney was doing better. The rainbow girl was still in a coma, but they'd moved her out of intensive care. "She's been breathing well on her own since we removed the respirator. Would you like to see her?"

Jennie nodded.

"She's in room 435, just down the hall, first door on the left."

The door was closed. Jennie pushed it open and stepped inside. It took a moment for her eyes to adjust to the darkness. She wondered why the lights were out. It seemed to Jennie that the nurses would want as much light as possible.

She felt along the wall for a switch, but didn't find it. Oh well, she didn't need a light anyway. She'd come up to see Courtney, but more than that, Jennie needed time to think and a quiet place to do it.

She left the door open to afford some light and moved deeper into the darkness. The first bed was empty.

Courtney's slender body occupied the one next to the window. The room was quiet except for the sound of Courtney's breathing—and hers. Jennie heard a faint scraping sound off to her right. The curtain moved, then parted. A dark, menacing shadow lunged at her.

23

Jennie raised her arm to ward off the blow. Whatever had been meant for her head hit her forearm. She staggered then fell to her knees as the figure pushed her aside and raced for the door.

Jennie hurt too much to scream. She hurt too much to do anything but lie there and moan. A moment later the overhead lights came on.

"What's going on?" The voice belonged to Brenda Stone, the nurse Jennie had talked to at the desk.

"I don't know," someone answered. "I was just coming out of 436 and saw some guy go out the stairs exit."

"You'd better call security." Brenda knelt beside Jennie. "Looks like this one's been hurt. Get a doctor up here stat."

"Courtney," Jennie gasped, trying to sit up. "I think someone was trying to . . ." Jennie moaned when the nurse touched her arm. Or maybe it was a scream. Her brain seemed oblivious to everything but the searing pain.

"I think her arm's broken. Otherwise she looks okay. She's moving on her own. Ken, help me get her on a gurney. If she's stable, have someone take her down to ER."

A strong pair of arms lifted her off the floor and deposited her on a narrow bed. "There you go. You'll be more comfortable here." Jennie winced as Ken placed a pillow under her arm.

"Angie," Brenda hollered. "Call a code. Get a crash cart in here quick."

The rails on both sides of Jennie snapped up into place. Ken wheeled her into the hallway. "Sorry about this," he said. "We'll have somebody here to take care of you in a minute. You just try to relax."

Relax? Someone had attacked her and run, which made Jennie fairly certain the culprit hadn't been paying Courtney a friendly visit. Had Courtney's attempted murderer come back? Had he succeeded this time?

One thing Jennie knew for certain—the person who hit her hadn't been Frank. The intruder had been smaller. Besides, the police had Frank in custody. Then who and why? The same one that had broken into the pharmacy? Jennie tried to tune out the throbbing pain in her arm and the scurrying hospital staff to concentrate on the attacker. She couldn't.

At least a dozen hospital personnel streamed into Courtney's room. All apparently responding to the official voice that droned over the intercom. "Code 99. Code 99. All available staff report to room 435 stat." The message was repeated three times, with no more emotion than a person would use to announce the items in a breakfast menu.

After what seemed an hour rather than five minutes, one of the nurses stopped to check on Jennie. "I'm sorry you have to wait. Are you in very much pain? I'll get you an ice pack."

The pain had settled to a dull agonizing ache between her wrist and her elbow. "That'd be great. Thanks. How is Courtney?"

"I really can't tell you that right now. But I'll try to let you know." The nurse left and came back with a towel-covered ice pack, which she placed on Jennie's arm.

The arm, Jennie noticed, had turned an angry shade of red and had swollen to about twice its original size. It looked like one of Popeye's, only crooked.

She pulled her knees up to take some of the pressure off her back and closed her eyes. As she began to relax the noise in the background dimmed. Like a bad dream, the scene in Courtney's room replayed itself in her head. As the intruder appeared, she felt something brush against her. She jumped, sending spasms of pain through her arm again.

"I'm sorry, I didn't mean to startle you." A young man in a white uniform gazed down at her. "I'm Adam Janzen, and if you're Jennie McGrady, I'm here to take you down to the emergency room."

"I can't leave now," she whined. As much as her arm hurt, Jennie didn't want to leave until she found out what had happened to Courtney. "I think someone tried to kill her. I need to know if she's going to be okay."

"I'll see if I can find anything out for you." Adam poked his head into room 435. A few seconds later he popped back out again. "You must have a weird imagination. According to one of the aids in there, your friend was having an insulin reaction."

Insulin reaction? "But . . ." Jennie stammered. "Courtney's not a diabetic—is she?"

"I wouldn't know." Adam maneuvered the stretcher down the hall and into the elevator. "All I know is they're talking medication error."

The next couple of hours went by in a blur of exams, X-rays, cast application, and what-am-I-going-to-do-with-you looks from Mom. While a technician applied a cast, a police officer took her statement of what had happened earlier in Courtney's room. Mom and Michael hung around with somber faces, trying to decide what to do with Mom's accident-prone daughter. They finally left after Jennie was safely tucked into a bed on the orthopedic ward with a guard posted outside her door.

The pain medication dulled her senses and sent her adrift in a state between wakefulness and sleep. For that reason,

Jennie couldn't be sure if what she'd seen had been for real or only a dream. Mom and Michael had been standing next to her, their arms around each other. He'd asked her to marry him, saying between the two of them they should be able to handle one slightly damaged teenager with a penchant for trouble. Jennie couldn't remember Mom's response.

———————

The first face Jennie saw when she woke up the next morning was Rocky's. His blue gaze was fastened on some papers. She smiled—or tried to. Her mouth felt like it had been sitting in a food dehydrator all night. "Hey, Rockford, we gotta stop meeting like this."

Rocky glanced up. He was obviously not amused. She braced herself for a lecture. It didn't come. "How's the arm?" he asked, setting his papers aside.

"Hurts," Jennie said. "What about Courtney? She okay?"

"She's stable. They moved her back into ICU. In fact, she's starting to come out of the coma. Doc says it's too soon to question her."

"The orderly told me she'd had an insulin reaction from a medication error. Is that what happened?"

His icy glare made her feel like a bug under a microscope. "I'll ask the questions, if you don't mind. You're going to have to stop trying to solve cases for us. Despite popular opinion, we do know what we're doing."

"Like I told the officer last night, I just went up to see Courtney. Only somebody else was already there."

"So I heard. We found a syringe on the floor with some of the insulin still in it. You apparently interrupted a murder. If you hadn't been there she may have died."

Jennie looked down at the cast on her arm and shrugged. "Glad I could help."

"Any idea who it might have been?" Rocky asked.

"I thought you didn't want me trying to solve crimes anymore."

"I don't. But you're a witness."

"I didn't see much. It was dark."

"But you did see something. Hair color? Height? Body type? Race? Clothing?"

"About my height and build. It happened so fast. That's about all I can think of."

"Did you know him?" Rocky's question caught her off guard. She hesitated a little too long. "You do, don't you?"

Jennie chewed on her lower lip. "I don't know who it is. All I can tell you is that he seemed familiar. I think it might be someone I know or have met."

"Was it your cousin's boyfriend?"

"No. Brad's much bigger than this guy." Jennie remembered something else. The insulin. Tina. Of course Tina hadn't been in the room, but it could have been one of her friends. No, Jennie reasoned. She'd been down that road before and it led to a dead end. Tina would have no reason to want Courtney dead. Jennie took a deep breath, wishing some of the puzzle pieces floating around in her brain cells would assemble themselves into some kind of order.

Rocky stood. "If your memory improves, give me a call."

"I will."

The doctor discharged Jennie that morning. Mom came to pick her up. They were halfway home before Jennie asked Mom about Michael. "Are you two back together?"

Mom's lips curled in a reluctant smile. "It looks that way. I've been doing some serious soul-searching over the last few days and realize I do love him. You were right."

"About what?"

"Remember what you said to me after we did that news conference—about you and I having to make adjustments and working things out?"

Jennie nodded.

"Well, don't let it go to your head, my darling daughter, but that was very wise counsel."

"Yeah?" Jennie grinned.

"So, yes, Michael and I are back together."

Jennie half smiled. It was good news—sort of. On the one hand she was happy for Michael and for Mom—on the other, she couldn't help wondering about Dad. And wishing the light in Mom's eyes could have been for him.

For two hours Nick and Hannah played doctor, with Jennie as their patient. For a while Jennie thought they were cute, sticking make-believe needles in her arm, poking Popsicle sticks in her mouth to take her temperature, and bringing real ice packs. When Nick asked Mom for a knife so he could do brain surgery, the game ended.

Michael came by around one and offered to take Nick and Hannah to the park. Jennie insisted Mom go along, which she finally did when Lisa showed up to keep Jennie company.

Once Mom, Michael, and kids were gone, Jennie sent Lisa into the kitchen to fix them some lemonade. Jennie went to her room to retrieve her suspect chart. Broken arm or not, she had to figure out who had attempted to kill Courtney for the second time.

Lisa, nearly back to her bubbly, exuberant self, had appointed herself Jennie's assistant.

With chilled, sweating glasses on the white wicker table and pillows to prop Jennie's arm up, she and Lisa sat on the porch swing and went to work.

"Now," Jennie began, "it stands to reason that whoever tried to kill Courtney last night at the hospital is the same one who beat her up."

"That makes sense. They didn't succeed the first time, so last night they tried again. But why didn't they try sooner?"

"Maybe they didn't see her as a threat before."

"Oh," Lisa's eyes brightened in understanding. "Because she's getting better."

"And because she was moved out of intensive care. In ICU, no one could get to her." Jennie handed Lisa the chart and asked her to hold it and make notes. "Having my right arm in a cast is definitely going to be a drag."

"Don't worry. I'll be your right arm for as long as you need me." Lisa grinned and struck a secretarial pose with pen and pad at the ready. "Where do we start?"

"Okay, I'm looking for suspects that could have been at both places and who fit the description of the person I surprised last night. It's someone who knew Courtney was a diabetic and who knew she was better. Which means we can cross Frank and Brad off the list."

Lisa drew a double wavy line through both names. "I know you're going to think I'm crazy, but I decided to give Brad another chance."

"Lisa. . . ."

Lisa held a hand up to silence her. "I know you think I should dump him, but I've made up my mind."

Jennie lifted her shoulders and let them fall. "Just be careful, okay?"

"I will." Lisa moved the pen down the list. "What about Tracy?"

Jennie closed her eyes and tried to visualize the figure in the dark room. "Tracy's too short, and I don't think she's strong enough to have done this." Jennie lifted her arm about two inches from the pillow and set it down again.

"On your chart you said she could have hired someone to beat Courtney up. If she did it once, she could do it again."

"True. The only thing is, if Tracy hired someone, why go back and finish up the job? She's already on rally squad. And she doesn't want Joel." Jennie sighed. "Leave her on for now." She wiggled her fingers, something the nurses had told her to do every once in a while.

"How come you don't have Joel on the list?"

"I didn't have time to finish it. But we'd have to cross him off now anyway. He has an airtight alibi for last night. He was still hooked up to a heart monitor in the coronary care unit."

"Who else did I write down?" Jennie asked, leaning over for a closer look.

"Gavin Winslow." Lisa looked up. "You can't be serious."

Gavin. As Jennie replayed the arm-breaking incident in her mind again, another memory imposed itself on the scene—the one of her standing next to Gavin at the window of Courtney's room.

No. Jennie refused to accept the possibility of Gavin's guilt. True, she'd penciled his name in on her suspect chart, but . . . Gavin was a friend. He cared for Courtney—Jennie had seen it in his eyes that day at the hospital and in the sensitive story he'd written about the rainbow girl—his rainbow girl. *Maybe he cared too much*, Jennie reminded herself. Courtney had dumped him for Joel. Hurts like that went pretty deep.

Suddenly it all fit. He knew Courtney was getting better. And in a brilliant move that would undoubtedly make her a laughingstock among amature sleuths, Jennie had filled him in on all the details, including the fact that the nurses would be moving Courtney out of ICU.

"Jennie? What's wrong?"

"Nothing. I . . ."

The phone rang, interrupting their conversation. Just as well. Jennie needed more time to process this new information before she could share it with anyone.

Lisa hurried in to answer the phone and came out less than a minute later. "It's Gavin. Says he needs to talk to you right away."

Jennie stood up and took a deep breath. On legs rubbery as gumbo, she went in to have a chat with the would-be murderer.

24

"No. Absolutely not," Rocky growled. "May I remind you, this is not a script for 'Murder, She Wrote.' And you are not Jessica Fletcher."

Jennie thought she'd handled the conversation with Gavin rather well. Her acting skills couldn't have been better. Her plan to catch the creep seemed impeccable. Unfortunately Rocky was demanding she change one of the scenes. Her idea had been to meet Gavin at his place. Gavin had told her he wanted to go to the hospital to see Courtney, but his bike tire was flat so he wanted her to pick him up.

Jennie saw through his story immediately. How could he think she'd be that naive? It upset her even more that she hadn't seen through his guise before. She agreed to meet him. Once there, she'd confront him with the evidence, he'd confess, then try to kill her. Of course, Rocky would be waiting off scene, rush in and save her.

Case closed. Rocky, spoilsport that he could be at times, had insisted she let the police handle it alone. After threatening to break her other arm if she tried anything foolish, Rocky hung up. So much for having a friend on the police force.

"Okay, maybe I did get carried away," she said, complaining to Lisa and getting no sympathy. "I just wanted to see the look on Gavin's face when I confronted him."

"Jennie McGrady, you're just mad because he conned you. You want to get even."

"I guess you're right," Jennie sighed. "I hate being wrong about people."

"You weren't totally wrong about him. You did have his name on the suspect list. Maybe that was your subconscious telling you he was guilty."

"Hmmph."

Jennie spent the next few hours resting and wondering what had happened with Gavin. Not that she expected the police to keep her informed of their every move. Still, she had hoped Rocky would let her know something. She'd begun to feel guilty about bringing the police in instead of meeting Gavin herself. Second, third, and fourth doubts surfaced and Jennie just wanted to be reassured that she'd done the right thing. *Of course you did, McGrady*, she told herself. *Gavin was definitely the guy in that hospital room. Definitely. Unless . . . stop it, McGrady. Just stop it.*

But the niggling memory of the person who'd been in Courtney's room lingered, and though the size and shape fit Gavin, something didn't. *The baseball cap.* Of course she wasn't certain that's what she'd seen, but Jennie's memory had brought forward the image of her attacker from a side view and she was almost certain he'd been wearing a cap. On the other hand, Jennie decided at last, Gavin could have worn a hat to throw suspicion off himself. Or not.

———

Lisa stayed for dinner and made plans to spend the night. After eating, Jennie and Lisa went up to her room. "How about brushing my hair, I'm having a hard time doing anything left-handed."

"Sure—I'll do a French braid. Your hair is perfect for that."

Lisa concentrated on Jennie's hair for the next few minutes. "How would you feel about going to the hospital to see Joel and Courtney tonight?" She sighed. "I haven't been to see either one of them. Guess I just couldn't stand being in the hospital again. Too many memories. I don't like being reminded of the stupid stunt I pulled."

It wasn't stupid, Jennie started to say, then didn't. Nearly killing herself to make the rally squad had been the dumbest move her cousin had ever made. "Sure," Jennie said. "But you'll have to drive."

Lisa and Jennie were about to leave for the hospital when the phone rang.

Lisa grabbed the receiver and handed it to Jennie.

"I need to talk to you, girl." Tina's voice faded in and out with a background of what sounded like cars on a busy street. She sounded out of breath—or frightened.

"What about?"

"Can't say. Jus' meet me at the park."

"Tina, are you all right?"

"No. Look, ya'll quit askin' questions and get on down here."

"Okay. Where are you?"

"Park Blocks."

"Yes, but where?"

"South end—by the college."

"Hang on, Tina, I'll be there as soon as I can." Jennie hung up. "Come on, Cuz. We're going for a ride. I'll explain on the way."

Jennie filled Lisa in on the runaway's strange phone call while Lisa drove.

"Why would she call you?"

"I'm not sure. Maybe she trusts me. All I know is that Tina's in trouble. She sounded scared and I can't help wondering if she's low on insulin."

"I wish I could park closer," Lisa said as she pulled up to the curb.

"This is fine."

"It's getting dark." Lisa stared into the trees and shadows that separated them from the area where Tina was supposed to be waiting. "I don't think we should go in there."

"We have to."

Jennie stepped out of the car, closed the door, and leaned in the window. "Stay here and wait for me. I'll take a quick look around. If I find her I'll bring her back to the car to talk. If I don't come back in the next five minutes, call the police."

"No." Lisa got out of the car. "I'll go with you."

They found Tina lying at the base of a tree. Only Tina wasn't saying anything. "I was afraid of this. I don't know that much about diabetes, but I do know they can die if they don't get insulin." Jennie tried to arouse her, but couldn't.

"Is she—"

"I don't know." Jennie felt for a pulse and found one. "Her pulse is weak. We passed a pay phone about a block west of here. Go call for help. I'll stay with her."

"Come on, Tina." Jennie lifted Tina into a sitting position after Lisa took off at a run. "Hang in there. We'll get you some help."

A figure stepped between Jennie and the setting sun. Jennie had the sinking feeling the person wasn't there to help. The menacing stance tipped her off, but the partly hidden gun solidified her notion.

"I don't think so, Jennie. She'll be dead before anyone can get to her. And so will you."

Jennie forced herself to stay calm. She raised her gaze from the gun barrel to the denim shirt to the baseball cap.

The scene from the night before slammed into her brain. This was the person she'd seen in Courtney's room. Tall and slender, like Jennie, only more muscular. *How could you have been so stupid, McGrady? The baseball cap. That should have clued you in immediately.* The family probably had dozens of them. Jennie doubted Gavin even owned one.

"You seem surprised. And here I thought you were such a good detective."

"I'd have figured it out soon enough."

"Yeah. That's what had me worried."

"How did you . . ." Jennie glanced down at Tina. "You had her call me? What did you do to her?" Jennie stood, ready to fight.

"I wouldn't try anything if I were you. I didn't hurt her. She did it all to herself—it's pretty stupid not to go to a doctor when you're out of insulin." She waved the gun. "Come on, let's go."

"I'm not leaving Tina."

Cassie shoved the cold steel into Jennie's ribs. "You'll go. Unless you want me to bring your cousin too."

That did it. Jennie allowed herself to be led back in the direction she and Lisa had come. "I don't get it," she said. "Why would you want to kill Courtney?"

"I didn't want to." Cassie opened a car door on the driver's side and pushed Jennie inside. "Don't get any ideas about running. I'm a good shot." Cassie hurried around to the passenger side and climbed in. She jammed the key in the ignition. "Start the car."

Jennie held up her casted arm. "I can't."

"Do it."

Jennie grasped the key and turned, gritting her teeth as a spasm of pain traveled up her arm. "I can't."

Cassie gave her a look of disgust and twisted the key. The engine started. Cassie shoved the automatic transmission into drive. "Let's go."

"Where?" Beads of perspiration formed on Jennie's forehead. Some from pain—most from fear.

Jennie used her left hand to maneuver the wheel and guided the car onto the one-way street. The traffic was light.

"Where are we going?"

"Just drive. I'll tell you when to turn."

"Since you're so intent on killing me, don't you think you could at least tell me why you're doing this?"

"You're the detective. You figure it out."

"It won't take long for the police to discover that Gavin didn't do it. Since you and I are about the same size too, I'd have eventually come around to you. But I don't get it. You said a few minutes ago you didn't want to beat up Courtney. . . ."

"I didn't."

The truth hit Jennie with the impact of a cement truck. "It was Joel. I should have guessed it. The way you protected him when you found out about the steroids. What happened?"

"Take a left on Lovejoy." The fact that Cassie didn't deny it told Jennie she'd guessed right.

Jennie angled off on Lovejoy, then onto Cornell Road and through the tunnels. A dozen scenarios of how she might escape marched through her brain. She dismissed all of them.

"Joel didn't mean to hurt her," Cassie said at last. "It was an accident. They got in an argument."

"And he beat her up."

"It was the steroids. They call it a 'roid rage. He thought he'd killed her. That night, after she talked to Brad, she went home. Brad called Joel and told him Courtney wouldn't be able to get them any more 'roids. Joel went to her house and . . ." She paused. "He was scared and didn't know what to do so he put her in the trunk of her car and called me. I told him to move his car a block or so away and come get me in her car."

"So it was your idea to throw her into a dumpster." Jennie shook her head. "But you didn't do that right away, did you? First, you had to plant the seed that she'd run away."

"It was the only way. I knew about Courtney's mom and the trial. With the blood in the trunk of her car, I figured they'd blame her dad."

"And you made sure by telling everyone Frank had abused her."

"Drive into the park," Cassie said.

"Why would you want to kill me? It won't help. Sooner or later Courtney's going to wake up and . . ."

"No. No she won't. And this time, you're not going to be around to stop me."

"Cassie, please. If you turn yourself in now, you'll be facing burglary and attempted murder charges. If you kill Courtney—and me, you'll . . ."

"Just shut up." She lifted the gun from her lap and pointed it at Jennie's head. "They're not going to find out."

"Why are you still trying to protect Joel? Everyone knows about the steroids."

"You just don't get it, do you? A lot of athletes use 'roids. They just manage to get away with it. Joel didn't. So, he'll get clean and maybe still be able to play pro ball in a couple of years. If word got out that Joel beat up Courtney it would be the end of our family. Joel would go to prison. My dad would lose his endorsements. He'd lose his job—we'd lose everything."

Jennie glanced at Cassie. She'd somehow convinced herself that she had to keep Joel's secret no matter what the cost. Reasoning with her wouldn't work. Jennie doubted she could take Cassie down. Even though they were close to the same height, Cassie was much stronger.

Your only chance is to outrun her, McGrady. Right. You may be fast, but only Superman and God can outrun a speeding bullet.

"Park over there." Cassie pointed to a parking area that led to a trail. No one would be walking it at night. If Cassie killed her it could be days before anyone found her body.

Jennie parked the car and left the keys in the ignition. She got out as Cassie instructed, then walked ahead of her. Jennie had outwitted a killer before, on a trail much like this one.

Jennie walked along in silence, waiting for the right moment. An owl hooted. Jennie stopped. Cassie closed the distance between them. Jennie slammed her left elbow into Cassie's stomach. She immediately swung around and brought her fist down on Cassie's wrist. The gun flew out of her hand and landed in the bushes. Jennie didn't wait around to find out if Cassie found it again. She raced back toward the parking lot. She climbed into the car and locked the doors, then twisted the key with her left hand.

She switched on the headlights and backed the car out of the parking space. Cassie emerged from the woods. She'd recovered the gun and raised it. Jennie ducked. The bullet ripped through the glass. She turned the wheel sharply to the left and hit the gas pedal. Raising her head just enough to see the road, Jennie tore out of the lot and up the road. She could barely see through the web of cracks that spread from the bullet hole across half the windshield.

Minutes later, Jennie drove into a gas station. On legs of rubber, she stumbled out of the car into a phone booth. She gave the police Cassie's description and location as well as her own, then hung up.

Instead of getting back into the car, Jennie leaned against the glass and metal booth and sank to the ground. She drew her knees to her chest and rested her throbbing casted arm on them and waited.

25

"I love happy endings," Lisa said as she balanced her food tray and gazed over the lunch crowd at Clackamas Town Center. "Courtney's awake and Tina's going to have a place to live. That really blew me away."

"You mean Mr. Evans agreeing to take her in?"

Lisa nodded. "I guess I shouldn't be so surprised. He was so glad to get Courtney back, he'd have promised her anything."

"What surprises me is that Tina agreed to live with them."

Lisa chuckled. "Poor Mr. Evans—can you imagine having Courtney and Tina in the same house?"

"One thing's for sure, it won't be dull."

Jennie spotted Gavin sitting alone at a small round table overlooking the ice rink. She nodded toward him and started walking his way.

"Hey," he said as Jennie and Lisa slid into the chairs opposite him. "I sure appreciate your agreeing to let my mom write about you. She's really excited." Gavin moved the Coke he'd just finished to the center of the table.

Jennie sat down and began nibbling on a French fry. "It's the least I could do. I still feel really bad about getting you arrested. Besides, she's a good writer. I loved her book."

"You don't need to feel bad about my being arrested. I

was pretty scared at first, but after a while I just told myself to calm down and take in all I could. Now I have the firsthand experience of being arrested. If I ever want to write about it, I know exactly how it feels."

"Well, I'm glad we can still be friends." Jennie smiled, grateful for his quick ability to forgive. She liked that about him. In fact, she liked a lot of things about Gavin. If she didn't care so much for Ryan, and if Gavin wasn't still crazy about his rainbow girl, she might even consider him boyfriend material. "I made a lot of enemies trying to solve this case."

Lisa shifted her green gaze from the turkey sandwich she was trying to eat, to Jennie. "You really shouldn't be so hard on yourself, Jen. You saved Courtney's life, and Tina's. And in the end, you solved the mystery."

"I guess." Jennie stuck a fry in a dab of ketchup. "Only it still feels all wrong. Cassie and Joel are just kids. Not that they're innocent. I mean, Joel did beat up Courtney and Cassie tried to cover it up."

"Cover it up?" Lisa grimaced. "That's putting it mildly. She tried to kill Courtney twice, broke into Evans' Pharmacy, knocked out your mom, and tried to kill you and Tina."

Jennie sighed. "I know. I'm not discounting her guilt— she'll have to serve time for what she did. It just seems to me the real crime in all of this is the adults like Coach Haskell and Mr. Nielsen who push kids to out-perform everyone else in sports."

"I'm with you, McGrady," Gavin said. "Joel and Cassie were pawns in a much bigger game. If anyone is ultimately to blame it's Joel's dad. Mr. Nielsen was disappointed in Joel's size and in his game. When Joel turned to steroids he got his dad's attention."

"Of course, some of the blame has to fall on Courtney," Jennie added. "She did supply the steroids."

"Under duress." Gavin leaned back in his chair and stretched his long legs out in front of him. "Courtney told me she never wanted to do it, but Joel and Brad convinced her it was okay. They even showed her an article where this German coach made his star athletes take steroids. She went along with it because she didn't want to let Joel down." Gavin closed his eyes and sighed. His Adam's apple bobbed up and down and Jennie wondered if he was going to cry.

"Have you heard any more about the charges against her?" Lisa asked.

"No." Gavin shifted forward, in control again. "The important thing is that she's awake and normal. She's been released into her dad's custody. She'll probably have to do community service time, but it looks like she's learned her lesson about supplying drugs—no matter how much a person might need it."

Lisa winced and stared at her unfinished fruit drink. "I didn't help matters. I wish now that I could go back and undo the damage I did."

"Seems to me," Gavin said as he pushed his glasses against his nose, "we'd all like to do things a little differently. Only we can't go back."

"But we can go forward." Jennie scrunched up her napkin and resolved to set the unpleasant case behind her. "Which reminds me, I'd better scoot. I promised Mom I'd be packed and ready to go tonight. We're flying out early tomorrow morning."

"Flying out?" Gavin raised his eyebrows. "Where are you going?"

"She gets to go to a dude ranch in Montana." Lisa pouted, stood, and tossed her empty cup in the trash. "I have to stay here. Mom thinks the trip would be too strenuous for me."

They set their trays on top of the food court's trash bins,

wove their way around the tables, and out into the main part of the mall.

"Maybe your parents will change their minds," Jennie said as they walked toward the exit. "I'll call them and tell them how healthy it is out there. All that fresh air and good food . . ."

Gavin glanced from one to another. "What—is this a vacation or something?"

"Not exactly. Mom got a letter from her sister, Maggie," Jennie began. "Her husband, Jeff White Cloud, is in the hospital. They had some kind of explosion that killed the foreman and badly injured Jeff. Anyway, they're at the height of the tourist season and Aunt Maggie needs help running the ranch."

"Where is it? I mean, Montana is a big state."

"The ranch is in western Montana near the Bitterroot Mountains," Lisa explained. "They call it *Dancing Waters*— isn't that a great name?" She sighed, her eyes huge and sad. "I'm so jealous. I love horses—and cowboys."

Jennie chuckled and draped an arm over Lisa's shoulders. "I'll check them out and let you know if it's worth the trip. Actually, I'm looking forward to seeing the llamas, *and* my cousins, of course."

"So, are you gonna solve the mystery?" Gavin asked.

"What mystery?"

"The bombing. I'm betting it's a terrorist act—those militia groups are big out there. Or maybe someone wants to cause your uncle a lot of trouble so he'll sell. Maybe he caught someone rustling cattle. Or, there could be silver or copper on the property. . . ."

"Whoa." Jennie tossed Gavin an incredulous look. "There's no mystery. I'm just going to help run the ranch until Uncle Jeff gets out of the hospital."

"Sure you are." Gavin winked at Lisa and gave her a knowing grin.

"Okay. I admit, I'm a little curious. Aunt Maggie did say the sheriff was investigating. And that some unusual things had been happening lately, but I'm not going out there to solve a mystery."

After saying goodbye, Jennie climbed into her Mustang and headed home. Excitement mounted with each mile. What would Montana really hold?